In the Night of Memory

In the Night of Memory

a novel

Linda LeGarde Grover

University of Minnesota Press
Minneapolis
London

Published by the University of Minnesota Press
111 Third Avenue South, Suite 290
Minneapolis, MN 55401-2520
http://www.upress.umn.edu

ISBN 978-1-5179-0650-4 (hc)
ISBN 978-1-5179-0651-1 (pb)

A Cataloging-in-Publication record for this book is available from the Library of Congress.

Printed in the United States of America on acid-free paper

The University of Minnesota is an equal-opportunity educator and employer.

24 23 22   10 9 8 7 6 5 4 3 2

To the missing Native women
and all who grieve them

Tho' you are singing somewhere still
I can no longer hear you.

— LEONARD COHEN

Contents

Gakina Awiya—
All Who Are Here

bound by blood, by name, by love, by spirit

to Loretta Gallette and her daughters, Azure Sky and Rainfall Dawn

**LAFORCE RELATIVES AND FRIENDS OF
MOZHAY POINT RESERVATION LANDS**

Family of Marguerite LaForce

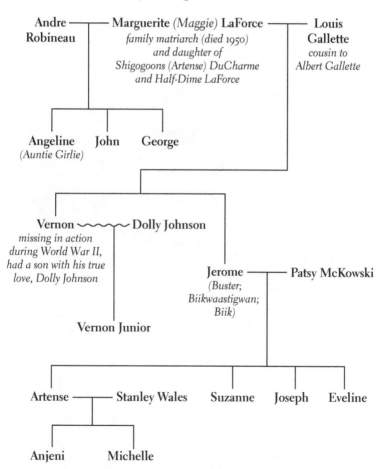

**Andre
Robineau** ——— **Marguerite** *(Maggie)* **LaForce** ——— **Louis
Gallette**
family matriarch (died 1950)   *cousin to*
and daughter of   *Albert Gallette*
Shigogoons (Artense) DuCharme
and Half-Dime LaForce

Angeline **John** **George**
(Auntie Girlie)

Vernon ⌇⌇ **Dolly Johnson**
*missing in action
during World War II,
had a son with his true
love, Dolly Johnson*

Jerome ——— **Patsy McKowski**
*(Buster;
Biikwaastigwan;
Biik)*

Vernon Junior

Artense ——— **Stanley Wales** **Suzanne** **Joseph** **Eveline**

Anjeni **Michelle**

Other LaForce Family and Friends

Earl LaForce, *Maggie's brother*

Margie Gallette, *cousin to Artense*
  Crystal Washington

Fred Simon, *Sweetgrass representative
to the Mozhay Point tribal government*
  Freddie-Boy Simon, *Fred's son*

Joseph Washington *(Zho Wash)*
  Michael Washington, *Zho Wash's son*

Beryl Robineau Dulebohn *married* **Noel Dulebohn**

Grace Hubert Dionne, *who is from the South, married* **Roy Dionne**
  Dale Ann Dionne *married* **Jack Minogeezhik**

Pearl Ricebird Minogeezhik *married* **Frank Minogeezhik**
  Jack Minogeezhik *married* **Dale Ann Dionne**

Boy Dommage
  Lucy Dommage, *Boy Dommage's daughter*

Annie Dommage, *Boy Dommage's cousin*

GALLETTE RELATIVES AND FRIENDS
OF THE MISKWAA RIVER SETTLEMENT

Albert Gallette *and* **Frances Dommage**
  Loretta Gallette
    Rainfall Dawn
    Azure Sky

Louis Gallette

Lisette Gallette Schoening, *sister to Louis Gallette*
  Babe Gallette Warner, *Lisette's daughter*

EXTENDED FAMILY AND FRIENDS IN DULUTH, MINNESOTA

Howard Dulebohn, *friend of Junior Gallette*

Rose *(Sis)* and **Florence Sweet,** *cousins to Gallettes; friends of Dolly*

Nolie Dulebohn, *grandson of Beryl Dulebohn*

FRIENDS FROM MINNEAPOLIS, MINNESOTA

Ingrum Viken
Winifred *(Winnie)* **Schmidt**

The Surrender
of Children

AZURE SKY

Our mother, Loretta, gave us the most beautiful names she could think of. She gave us a memory, one that I have told to Rainy so many times that to her it has become real—though I wonder if it never happened at all and is only one of my dreams. And when Rainy was four, and I was going on three, our mother gave us to the St. Louis County foster care system. It was the same year that Duluth's mining heiress Elisabeth Congdon was murdered by her daughter and son-in-law. The crime was spectacular, and although it happened decades ago now it is still talked about around town, and every time it comes up, I think of my mother. She and Miss Congdon, whose lives never intersected, are linked in this single way.

Rainfall Dawn and Azure Sky are our real names, the ones Loretta wrote down for our birth certificates, though she called us Rainy and Azure most of the time. When she wanted something, or was stressed, or had been drinking, or all three—Baby and Sister. Rainy was Baby because she was born first, and I was Sister because I came second, a year and a half later. Nobody has called us Baby and Sister since the morning Loretta was getting us ready to go on that cab ride to the County. We haven't seen her or heard from her since. I think. I am not sure.

Although Rainy and I have forgotten Loretta's face, Rain occasionally thinks she sees our mother in the gracefully bending woman at the butcher counter, whose long hair sweeps to the side as she looks at a tray of pork chops. She might see her in a traditional dancer wearing a dark blue calico dress at the Mozhay Point spring powwow who, turning to face the flags during Grand Entry, is in fact our Auntie Margie, or in the bundled-up homeless woman picking aluminum cans from the trash barrel at the bus hub in downtown Duluth.

I have forgotten our mother's voice, yet I still hear her husky whisper from the night she woke us to see the northern lights and watch her dance, and it is this memory that I choose for us to keep, whether it was just a dream or really happened. And so my mother still whispers to me: when it starts to rain and drops of liquid quench the thirst within the sparse leafiness of the old maple tree in the front yard, the wet patter deepening on saturated leaves, rolling water onto the dryness of exposed roots. She whispers to me in the absence of rain, on days that the wind picks up and scatters dried leaves across a sidewalk; in the braking of a city bus or in the weighty freedom of northern lights in the night sky. Sometimes I hear her all day and at other times not for months, and I think that she is gone for good after all. And then once again she whispers, and on the air grown warm and damp with her breath is what I had forgotten, the perfume of cigarette, the yeasty sweetness of white bread and red wine. *Azure . . . Azure Sky, Sister . . . Rainy . . . Rainy Dawn, Baby . . .*

The night of the memory I woke to our mother whispering through my dreams of a buffalo nickel glowing in the sky, its shine dulled through the flyspecked and finger-smudged windows. And through the fog of interrupted dreams, Rain, who slept on the other end of the couch, kicking me across the chest and asking, Is it morning, Mama?

Rainy . . . Rainy Dawn, Baby . . . I would recognize the sound of her voice today if she sat behind us on the bus. It is a young voice that I remember, lightly husky with just the start of cigarette smoke settling tar into her throat. Today, it would be lower in pitch, I suppose, but I would know the urgency and loneliness of our mother's solitary life and plaintive speech. Would she remember who we were, Rainy small and Azure tall? Would she recognize what we have become, two halves of one sister?

Our mother, if she is still alive, would recognize us. There is no doubt about it, she would recognize us. She is our mother after all; of course she would. From the bus seat behind mine and Rainy's she might see only the backs of our heads but would know us anywhere. She would remember the color of Rainy's hair, the darkest brown shot through with red highlights, this morning combed and parted by me exactly down the middle. Rainy is so short that in turning my head I can see the entire top of hers, where her braids have been crossed and tightly pinned from ear to ear. Where her hair is parted, her vanilla-caramel skin is slightly reddened from the sun. My own hair, a cloudy brown as dark as Rain's although not as red, waves and sways from its high ponytail with the movement of the bus; I am so tall that it clears the bus seat and brushes the hand that our mother lifts to touch the back of my shoulder as she says our names in her voice that is now older, rougher. I turn toward her voice and the perfume of her warm breath, the cigarette smoke and yeasty red wine, and because she was never really there, she is gone.

We haven't seen her since that morning of our surrender. Rainy, who sees impossible sights, sees our mother everywhere.

I listen for it, and when in the sound of rain on dry leaves she whispers our names, I turn.

The front room where we slept had no curtains, and all through the night the street lamp outside shone onto the couch where we lay, one on each end. I slept on my back with one forearm across

my face to block the light. Rainy slept in a C-shape with her face
turned toward the back of the couch, her knees pressing against my
side and her backside sticking out into the room. Sometimes she
rolled and fell off. To this day it comforts me to lie on my back, with
one arm across my face, and that is how I fall asleep. Sometimes
during the night, if I have changed from that position, she whispers
from somewhere, perhaps from a corner of the room, *Rainy Dawn,
Baby . . . Azure Sky, Sister . . .*

Her whisper wakes me and I am returned to the front room
of our apartment, where Rainy is four and I am going on three.
From the back of the apartment a door slams; bare feet brush bare
wooden floors toe to heel, and that is how I know it is our mother
because that is the way she dances, toe to heel, and the way she
walks from the kitchen to the front room. Since it is the middle of
the night, I am afraid. What woke her and what could she be looking for? What dreadfulness follows and chases our mother through
the apartment in the middle of the night, causing her to wander
from her bedroom to the front room and then the kitchen, checking the doors to ensure that they are locked, fretting and muttering, pacing, translucent under the moonlight and streetlight in her
white T-shirt and gray sweatpants? Loretta, who I reach out from
my end of the couch to touch as she passes and wonder if perhaps
she is not really there at all but only a continuation of my dreams of
weeping, wandering ghosts and a ghost, herself.

The night of the memory, the ghost who is really our mother en-
ters the front room, blocking the glare from the street lamp; Rainy
wakes on the other end of the couch and, kicking me across the
chest, asks, Is it morning, Mama?

"No, no; it's still the middle of the night, but you have to see
this." She wraps the blanket that we share around Rainy and picks
her up because Rain is so small and easy to carry. She takes my
hand. "Azure, are you awake? Come on, big girl, come to the back
porch and see."

The back porch is the fire escape off the door from the kitchen. Through the window over the kitchen sink I can see that the sky from the back of the apartment building is bright, not streetlight bright but a silvery glow that, advancing from the north, changes the edge of the sky from green to purple. I'm afraid, but *Come on, come see*, our mother says, and is it trust or a leap of faith? We follow her out the kitchen door to the small fire escape, a landing large enough for one man, but the three of us just fit. Our mother takes the blanket she has wrapped around her own shoulders and spreads it on the wooden floor; she wraps the other blanket over the three of us.

"Waawaate," she says. "Waawaate; it's the northern lights."

Wrapped in blankets we share body warmth as well as our body scents that rise from where the blankets open just below our necks: my mother's perspiration of yeasty white bread and red wine and fearful grief; Rainy's faint steaminess of urine and hair that our mother plans to wash in the morning; my acrid uneasiness mixed with the staleness of jeans that have been worn and slept in and worn again. We are nearly hypnotized by the shifting lights: Rainy's face is tipped up toward them, her opal eyes changing colors silver to green to purple with the lights; her mouth is open and smiling slightly; her small broken teeth, blackened and crooked, are ghostly in the night. Mother is ghostly, too; her face is a reflection of the lights. She rises, and I am again frightened but draw up from my shaky bowels my trust, or again, a leap of faith. She is Mother, she knows what she is doing, I tell myself without words, in the inarticulate way of small children.

"Biizindan, little sweethearts; shhhh . . . Can you hear them?" Pulled close, closer, our heads lift like our mother's to listen to the low rumble that is the singing wind of Waawaate. Rising, Loretta pulls the edges of the blanket from the floor and wraps them around me and Rain, then turns to face the lights. She sways, and then she is dancing in the style of Ojibwe traditional women, hands on hips and feet kneading the fire escape floor, its boards softened with age and weather, pivoting half-circles left to right, right to left, lifting the invisible eagle feather fan in her left hand to return the song of prayer that is the Creator-given gift of Waawaateg.

Rainy reaches for my hand and slides hers under mine, the way she would back then, when she was four and I going on three, just the same way she does today. In the warmth of the blanket and the stillness of the night air we fall asleep, eyelids closing slowly, because there is all the time in the world to watch our mother dance with the northern lights.

The County had determined that Loretta's surrendering of her children was an occasion that merited a taxicab. It was that determined merit, as well as the lessening of the chance that Loretta might renege or bolt on the way to Social Services should she be allowed to make her own way there, that brought the garnet-colored Buick, with *Norman's Taxi Service* stenciled in script on the sides, to the curb in front of the apartment building.

Anticipating the possibility of delays in getting Loretta and the children into the cab, Norman had arrived ten minutes early; he had done this before. He sat for a few minutes in his immaculately clean cab, with its pleasant scent of tobacco and pine, waiting for the client to see him if she looked out the window, before he would go to knock at the door. Sometimes that seemed to help, in Norman's experience; most of the time it at least didn't seem to make things any worse. Most of the time. He opened the driver's side window and lit a Marlboro.

Inside the apartment Loretta, who had been up for nearly a half-hour, gagged slightly as she stuffed a heavy, overfilled disposable diaper into the bottom of a brown paper bag of trash under the kitchen sink. Most mornings she pretended sleep as long as she could, eyelids clenched shut and wrinkled as she listened for whispers, tumbling on the couch, the opening and closing of the refrigerator door, small voices arguing, and then, finally, two small girls looking at her, she could feel it—Rainy, older but still in diapers, and younger but taller Azure, who had worried and fretted since the minute she was born. Then Rainy would lose interest while Azure would still be staring, then asking Loretta if she was awake, tentatively at first then insistently over and over and eventually tapping her head until, Loretta was ashamed to admit even to herself, she occasionally slapped her own baby girl. This morning might have been like one of those times, but instead Loretta slept hard, blessedly dreamless and oblivious to the sounds of children waking and stirring, then asking was she awake yet and could they have something to drink, something to eat? She had finished the inch or so of Chianti left in the jug before she went to bed the night before, and so after an hour or so of sleep had awakened and been awake off and on for most of the night, watching the clock and finally falling asleep again sometime after 4:00. And so Loretta didn't hear the alarm, overslept, and awoke to the sound of small voices and with not enough time to wash up the kids. And now the three of them had ten minutes left of the life that Rainy and Azure had no reason to think might be changing.

Opening the front room window in order to clear out some of the smell from the diaper, Loretta saw the beautifully shined cab pull up to the curb in front of the apartment building ten minutes early and moved away from the window unseen, she hoped, by the driver. As far as he was concerned, she wasn't home and didn't have to be until 8:45; until then Azure Sky and Rainfall Dawn were still hers. And as far as they knew, this morning was like any other, and the girls would wander the apartment as they had every morning for as long as their short baby memories could remember, which would be five months in real, adult, Loretta time. Loretta watched

the driver extend an arm out the window and tap ash from a cigarette to the street. The passenger side window opened; strains of
Nat King Cole drifted to the apartment's open window as he waved
cigarette smoke from the cab's interior with a folded newspaper.
The driver tapped the horn, twice.

After waiting another five minutes for Vicki Lawrence to finish
singing "It Must Be Him," he tapped it twice again and then got
out of the car, extinguishing the cigarette in his palm and tucking
it behind his ear as he walked quickly up the sidewalk and took the
outside stairs two at a time, an older man long-legged, spiderlike
in his movement and very thin. At the building's entryway, out of
Loretta's sight but not her hearing, he tried the front door, opened
it. Inside, grit on unswept tile crunched under his feet; when he
reached the stairway to apartment 2A, the sound muffled to a hol-
low toll of wooden-heeled and leather-soled cowboy boots, mournful on balding, carpeted steps.

His knock was four solemn beats. A wait, a clearing of his throat.
Four more solemn beats. Loretta listened; his breathing, an old
man's, heavy from the stairs.

"Somebody's at the door, Mama!" Rainy, sputtering her S's.

He would have heard Rainy; she would have to let him in. They
each had their instructions from the County, his to help her carry
luggage, hers to cooperate if she didn't want the police called.

Loretta opened the door, and the odor from cooking, sleeping,
and the diaper at the bottom of the brown paper bag under the sink
rolled out into the hall. The man didn't seem to notice the smell
or the mess; instead, he politely removed his hat. "Norman's Cab.
What do you need me to take, missus?" he asked her, as if she were
a regular paying customer who might tip.

*Rainy tells me that she doesn't remember any of this, but one
day she might, all of a sudden, the way she French-braided her hair
ten years later, when Dolly took us to the beauty school, as if she
remembered how to do it from one of her previous lives. I think that*

somewhere inside of her mind, our previous life with our mother and
our surrender is as real as if it is happening right now. Just as it is to
me, Azure. I remember; it is a memory and it is real, both at the same
time. I am in her bedroom half-hiding.

Loretta nods toward the corner next to the door. "Those two
things," she answers the driver.

I don't want to get out from under the bed.

"Azure Sky, come out of there, Sister; time to go."

Loretta had intended to wash the girls up really good at the
kitchen sink, because the shared bathroom was down the hall and
she didn't like to see or talk to the other tenants who wanted to get
in, the always pin-curled elderly woman who would ask again if
it was her kids who peed on the seat and could she remember to
watch for that and clean it up because nobody likes a dirty bathroom, or the overweight man who carried a bottle of Lysol with him
and wiped the doorknob down with a rag before he touched it but
who didn't put the seat down after and didn't always flush. And the
bathtub, pitted porcelain so stained you couldn't tell which streaks
were already there and which smears might have been new, and
you didn't want to find out by using it.

She had intended to wash their hair, to brush it until it shone—
Rainy's dark brown with those red highlights and Azure's springy
waves—and then comb and section and braid so smoothly and per-
fectly that the people at the County might say, "There must be a
mistake here. Anybody can see that their mother takes good care of
them." And they would return to the apartment, perhaps even in
another cab ride, all three. The County would leave them alone,
and the old lady in pin curls would tell Loretta that she was a good
mother, and the fat man with the bottle of Lysol would report to the
landlord what quiet, well-behaved children Loretta had, no trouble
at all and a pleasure to live next door to. The folks from Mozhay
Point would come to visit, and Auntie Beryl would remark on how
nice Loretta kept the apartment. Loretta would finish school, go to

college, become a teacher, and her girls, growing up, would have nice teeth and pretty clothes.

And then she overslept.

Well, they were dressed, anyway. Loretta bent Rainy's pot-bellied little body into a faded red corduroy jumpsuit, the tiny girl's wrists and ankles flexing compliantly in her hands. She smoothed the knots of fine auburn and brown hair that had tangled into an egg-sized wad at the back of Rainy's head as she slept.

"Want help with the kiddies, too, Missus?" the cab driver asked, as though he thought she was Queen Elizabeth. Rainy went right to the man, held her arms out to be lifted up onto his hip, wrapped her legs around his waist. Loretta directed him to carry the cardboard box that she had folded, flap over flap, across the top.

"Give me a minute." She ducked into the kitchen and quickly ate a slice of bread, this to settle and weight her stomach and absorb the smell of wine on her breath. The bread rose, rose, backing up; Loretta swallowed again, hard, and it stayed down. She breathed into a cupped hand, inhaled. Yeasty, fruity, not too winey, she decided, and returned to the front room, where Norman was holding Rainy with one arm and the cardboard box under the other.

"All right, let's go." Loretta picked up her leather suitcase, the kind that used to be called a grip.

"I'm hungry, Mama." Azure said this in the same whiney voice she used to ask if Loretta was awake, those mornings just before she had slapped her, Loretta recalled, which caused tears to drip down the back of her throat onto the slice of bread, which they salted. She swallowed both and pulled the last of the bread, the heel, from her pocket and handed it to her younger, bigger girl.

"I'm hungry too, Mama." Rainy reached for the bread, starting to cry when Loretta slapped her hand. Azure tore a piece from the heel and held it out to Rainy, who dropped it onto the floor. Loretta dug between the couch cushions for Rainy's pacifier, which her smaller, older girl slid between her lips and began to chew.

The man is kind to me, calls me little lady. I want to sit in front but he tells me I need to sit by my mother. I tell him what I had heard Loretta tell the landlord: we're going for a ride, that we're not gonna live with our mama no more. Sitting next to Mama I kick the seat back of the driver's seat. He doesn't say anything. Loretta, holding Rainy, moves my foot and takes my hand. Her own hand is damp and hot, and the nails are chewed. The cab smells nice; there is a little cardboard pine tree hanging from the radio knob. He asks if we are warm enough back there, says he can turn up the heat. Rainy falls asleep in minutes; the pacifier falls out of her mouth. Loretta opens up a tube of Life Savers and tells me I have to have the pine-apple because it won't leave my face stained.

Loretta remembered that she hadn't brushed her teeth and rubbed her sleeve across them. She wondered how she looked. *Too late now.* She put the thought of her teeth out of her mind and read the taxi license. Norman McNeil was the owner-operator, it said.

"He owns his own cab," she thought to herself. "No wonder the outside is so shined up and the inside so clean." The mingled scents of cigarette, Norman's leather jacket, and the little green cardboard tree hanging from the radio knob were as smooth as the ride's feel of good tires on blacktop. Norman's radio was turned to an oldies channel that he hummed along to in a deep rumble so low it might have been the engine, except that Loretta could recognize the tunes. The heater hummed with Norman, blowing air that warmed her feet, and she relaxed, thinking that she could ride there forever listening to Perry Como and Norman and watching the West End and then downtown sliding smoothly past the side window. "Can you girls see the lake?" she was going to ask, but before she had a chance the cab turned left and up the avenue to the civic center, where it stopped in front of the County building.

"I'll get the doors for you, Missus," the man says, but although my mother swings her legs down to the pavement she seems unable to get up. He offers her his hand, which she grabs, rising with Rainy in her

arms. He reaches back into the car for the handle of the grip; with a grunt he hoists the cardboard box up under the other arm. "Come on out, little lady," *he says to me; I take his hand, which he gently removes to place in my mother's. We walk, almost like a family, up the sidewalk and stairs and through the double glass doors of the County building where we are met by the social worker, who can smell the wine on Loretta and the diaper, old cooking, and sleep on me and Rainy and looks disgusted. She takes Rainy from our mother's arms and stands her on the floor, then takes my hand from my mother's. Rainy's arm, thin-boned inside her red corduroy jumpsuit, brushes mine and stays there.*

Loretta told the social worker that she would be back as soon as she had taken care of things at the hospital. "After I finish treatment, I'm getting my tubes tied, then I get my babies back," she said and wrote down her address and her cousin Artense's on the back of a drugstore receipt. She held the receipt out until the social worker took it. "You can bring the babies to Artense's if I'm not home, but you'll have to call first," she said. "Don't forget; the addresses are right here. The hospital will let you know when I'm out."

Norman figured the mileage and fare on a small billing tablet, tore it out, and gave it to the worker, who accepted it more willingly than she had the drugstore receipt with the instructions about Artense. "Thanks, Missus," he said to Loretta, nodding to her children. "It's a pleasure," he said, without a smile. As he walked, smoothly spiderlike, back to the cab he paused to pull the cigarette from back of his ear and a book of matches from his jacket pocket, turning and bending to shield the match from the wind as he lit up. Then he got into his cab and drove away.

Loretta kissed her children. As the social worker brought Azure Sky and Rainfall Dawn to the elevators and pressed the Up button, Loretta waved at them. Then the elevator doors opened, the social worker took the little girls inside, and pushed a button.

"Hurry up, Mama, the door's gonna close," the smaller girl said.

The taller girl took a step towards the mother.

"Be careful," the social worker said as she tightened her grip on both sisters' hands.

Loretta kept waving until the elevator door slid closed. And then she was alone.

Outside the glass doors she looked for a rock to throw at the civic center fountain; seeing none she grabbed the handle of the trash can next to the County building doors, ready to pull it across the drive and up over the edge of the sidewalk and into the water. As she set foot into the street an oncoming car braked, the driver tapping the horn twice; looking up, Loretta saw Norman's taxi circle back to the civic center and the County building.

Norman offered her a ride. "It's free," he said. "Got to go back that way anyway; no trouble at all."

Loretta was silent during the ride back to the apartment; noticing a small handprint on the side window she touched it gently, then rubbed it away with her jacket sleeve. Norman spoke twice, asking, when the cab was stopped at a red light, if she would like a stick of gum and then offering, after humming along with Doris Day, that "Que Sera, Sera" was his favorite song.

Pulled up at the curb in front of Loretta's apartment, Norm handed Loretta a ten-dollar bill. "Get yourself some groceries," he said. "There's a brighter day out there."

Inside the apartment building the day was, as Norman had predicted, brighter. The window shade on the usually dark landing had been raised, and bright sunlight shone on the man who knelt at Loretta's doorway. The landlord turned at the sound of her step, then silently continued to change the lock set.

Loretta pivoted and ran, down the stairs and out the front door of the apartment building, down the sidewalk and into the street, where she chased the maroon cab, waving her arms until it turned the corner and disappeared. She stopped running; a car honked and she moved to the curb.

On the sidewalk, a young man waiting for his dog to finish urinating against a dead elm tree hawked and spit on the sidewalk.

"Mornin'," he said to the woman who was holding her side and muttering, *Shit, shit.*

"Pig," said Loretta. "You ever think somebody's little kids might walk on this sidewalk?"

Then she walked back towards downtown, the ten-dollar bill a sweating mass wadded into the center of her fist.

Miskwaa

AUNTIE GIRLIE

I was thinking all yesterday. All afternoon and through supper and my programs on TV, right up to my bedtime, though not once my head hit the pillow because I sleep like a sack of rocks. Always have. It was yesterday that Nolie Dulebohn, that would be my cousin Beryl's grandson, well, he does the *Mozhay Masine'igan*, the reservation newsletter that comes out once a month, and he came to Elder Housing for lunch. He wanted to interview me because I am the oldest Mozhay elder. By far (I am adding this part myself). He wanted to know about the old days, which all the younger people like to read about because they are so different from things today that to them Mozhay in those times might have been like living on the planet Jupiter.

Elder Housing is a nice place, and I am glad to live here, on the ridge that runs along the southern shore of Lost Lake. There is a nice view here out of every one of our rooms, and out of the dining room, too, where Nolie ate every scrap of his macaroni and cheese and half of mine while I talked. The portions are not enough for younger people, and because Nolie can't ever hang on to his money, I think he probably didn't have enough to buy a second

19

lunch for himself. He ended the interview by asking me the secret to a long life. When people ask me that, they are really asking me why in the world I am not dead yet, and I mean this in a good way.

"Whiskey and cigars," I answered, which made him laugh, but then I told him what these oshki-Pointers would expect to read in the *Masine'igan*, that every morning the first thing I do is thank God for making me an Indian and then try my best to walk the path of Bimaadiziwin, the traditional Anishinaabe way of living a good life. Then Nolie packed up his laptop computer that he was taking notes on, shook my hand in a thoughtfully gentle way that didn't hurt my fingers, which are sore and strangely crooked with the arthritis, and said it was an honor to interview me (*Before you die, which could be any minute,* I could tell he was thinking).

The truth is, of course, that I don't smoke cigars, and I don't drink, at least not in the way my mother Maggie and her sister Helen did, though I do like a glass of wine while I watch my programs. The reason I have lived longer than anyone, even Beryl's husband, Noel, who was older than sin, is because I never married. Nobody ever asked me or even showed interest; I was never chosen and so my heart never took the beating that other women's do. Maggie's held out as long as it could, but between my father and then Louis, and then her children and all the Mozhay and Duluth relatives, it wore out when she was just sixty. Mine is still beating, steady and slow, never subject to the highs and lows of emotions, the long-term sorrowful slowing and abrupt jarring of the joys and frights that people like Maggie experienced. My secret to a long life is also my secret to a clear head and memory: I am untouched and bear no scars on my heart that beats as slow and cold-blooded as a turtle's. The Creator blessed me in this; it's a gift.

Although it is not by blood, although she is a Gallette and I am a Robineau, Loretta and I are related in the Indian way. Her father, Albert Gallette, and Louis Gallette were cousins, and my mother

Maggie and Louis's sons, Vernon and Buster Gallette, were my half-brothers. As Loretta's auntie in the Indian way, I will tell you that there is more to Loretta's story than her disappearance and more to her disappearance than the story. Stories like Loretta's were and are sadly so common that it didn't even merit mention in the news, that an Indian woman who lived a rough life had lost her children to the County and dropped off the face of the earth without anyone even noticing for the longest time. Loretta was one of those women, one of how many we will never know, and just as it was with Loretta it was for them, that the story is more than any individual lost woman's failings, more than speculation about the mystery, surely more than rumor and gossip and any satisfaction that it was her own fault, or that what goes around comes around, that you reap what you sow, that people get what they deserve. It's our history, the loss of land, of course, but there's more to it: the Old Indians, they knew how to live in the good ways but then so much became lost, with everything that was happening—people getting moved all over the place, the Indian schools and the families that lost their children, and then the drinking, the wrecking of lives—it leads directly to all that is Indian Country today, including the disappearance of Indian women, who the Creator intended to be the heart and spirit, the continuity of the people. That includes Loretta.

The Gallettes at Miskwaa River hadn't been in touch with Loretta since the last time she had left for Duluth, for Louis Gallette's funeral. She lived in Duluth for a while after that, where, if the rumor is true, she had a baby boy that she never saw because it was adopted out; it is where she lived when a couple of years later her first little girl Rainfall Dawn was born, then up north in Mesabi, she had her second, Azure Sky. Sometime after that she moved to Minneapolis, then back and forth between Minneapolis and Duluth so many times nobody ever kept track of where she was. It was in Duluth that she lost her children to the County; by the time people began asking if anybody had heard anything from Loretta lately, she was nowhere to be found, and her little girls had been lost, or hidden, somewhere within the foster system.

Miskwaa is a hard place to live. Miskwaa Ziibens is what it used to be called, the little red river that runs along the western edge of the Mozhay Point Reservation, a hundred miles or so north of Duluth. The name sounds pretty—doesn't it?— the little red river, and it is a beautiful place out there in the bush of rocky riverbanks and wild forest. Two hundred years ago fur traders and Indian trappers negotiated their business deals on the banks of a natural harbor below the rapids; a settlement grew around the trading post. When the fur trade failed and the post was abandoned, Waabishkaa Waboos and his son Half-Dime LaForce moved into the building, which they used as a trading place and store for the settlement and the Indians, lumberjacks, and homesteaders in the area. An able trader and skilled woodsman, eligible bachelor Half-Dime was married at a young age to Artense DuCharme the half-breed daughter of a lumber company clerk, a business arrangement that was lucrative for everyone, even the initially reluctant but heavily dowered Artense.

In the early 1890s, this would have been right around when my mother, Maggie LaForce, was born, the Mozhay Point Reservation Lands were divided into allotments, acreage that was assigned to band members, except for the half-mile-wide Miskwaa settlement along the eastern bank. That land was set aside for unallotted, displaced Indians who had no place to go because the allotted Mozhay Pointers were moving in. Half-Dime, as a signer of the treaty, was allotted forty acres near Lost Lake, which meant that the LaForces had to close up their store at Miskwaa Ziigens and move; the Lost Lake families, the unallotted Indians, relocated to the riverbanks. The unallotted Muskrat family, whose name was changed by the Indian agent to Washington, had to move from where they had been living, which was now assigned to the LaForces; displaced, they were the first to move to the eastern banks of the Miskwaa.

They were shortly joined by the Ricebirds, Etiennes, Dommages, Beavers, and Gallettes (who were double-cousins to the Dionnes but had not signed the treaty). They were all promised that they could stay on the Miskwaa River banks until the government should decide they would have to leave. This never happened, and as unrecognized Indians, the little Miskwaa River community and its people were forgotten by the federal government, by the Mozhay Point Reservation Indian agent and, sad to say, by the Mozhay Point band members much of the time, too. Those displaced Miskwaa River people lived on the trapping and harvesting that a half-mile riverbank strip provided, on welfare checks from the county, and the liquor trade, since liquor sales were illegal at Mozhay Point.

When Loretta Gallette was born, the ragged little Miskaa River settlement, if you could call it that, consisted of scattered tar-papered houses of one to three rooms, most without plumbing or electricity, and a one-room post office and general store added onto the original Etienne house by Kiiwizens Etienne, the old man of the family, who had been born in the bedroom. Mail was delivered via a contracted star route once a week; Mary Etienne, the postmistress, paid the star route driver extra to deliver supplies from Mesabi with the mail. The Etiennes had become the most prosperous family at Miskwaa, and the Dommages and Gallettes the heaviest drinkers. Loretta's father, Albert Gallette, cousin to Louis Gallette and my mother Maggie LaForce's second husband in the Indian way, which meant not through the Church; my father was Andre Robineau, Maggie's first husband. So again, although it is not by blood, I am related to Loretta. In the Indian way.

I am telling you all of this not to make excuses for anyone but so that you can understand how the past has an influence on the present and, in fact, never goes away.

At first, after their removal, the Miskwaa River Indians were very old-time in how they lived; today we would call them "traditional," but that word is somewhat misleading. It is true that the people there practiced the old-style religion and customs, that they hunted, fished, riced, and maple-sugared, and they continued the custom of dividing up the meat after a kill so that each of the families was fed. And although they still spoke the old-style Ojibwe language in their everyday lives, that language that should have reinforced all that was desirable in living in the ways of the old Anishinaabeg, the trials of life were simply too much for the Miskwaa River outcasts. The treaty Indians, who became known as the Mozhay Pointers, had gotten the better deal because of their land allotments: they became property owners, free to lose their land through swindle or theft, but property owners nonetheless. As for the people banished to the Miskwaa River banks, well, the pride their grandparents had taken in not admitting defeat by signing their homeland away resulted in their relocation and in their not owning anything at all, as a tribe or individually, except for the little houses they put up by themselves and might or might not be able to stay on the next day, or the next year. The treaty-signing Mozhay Pointers had prospered, the unallotted Miskwaa River Anishinaabeg had not: cold, hungry, and sick as they were, we could hardly blame them for neglecting the sacred teaching of generosity, tested as it was by hardship as well as the distances in land and legal standing between them and the treaty Indians, the Mozhay Pointers.

So, I am telling you this in case you were thinking that Miskwaa River, isolated like that, must have been like one of those hippie communes of the 1960s, free children of nature skipping around all happy through the woods and skinny-dipping in Miskwaa Ziibens. Their lives were hard, hard; they scrabbled for food and to stay alive during the winters. They were only human. Rough though their lives became, their pride was their history and their use of the old-time Ojibwe tongue and continuation of the old religious practices and customs. They considered themselves to be the "real" Indians, and the Mozhay Pointers considered them that, too. But the Miskwaa River people, the unallotted Indians, in spite of their pride and their best intentions, were unable to hold on to everything, and much that was precious to them eroded.

You can see it was complicated, and in one way they were simply unlucky, in the wrong place at the wrong time. They were not completely forgotten by the federal government, because of the Indian agent, whose job it was to report on the Native communities of his assigned region, which did not stop at the western boundary of the Mozhay Point Reservation. The Miskwaa River families—and those were big extended families of lots of relatives, unallotted and denied the fruits of reservation status, such as they were, enjoyed by the Mozhay Pointers—were nevertheless recognized as Indians in that their children, too, were removed from their families around the age of five or six and sent away to Indian boarding schools: Pipestone, Vermilion Lake, St. Veronique, Red Lake Government, Red Lake Mission, Tomah, St. Mary, Flandreau, Haskell, and finally, Harrod, which is where most of the Mozhay Point and Miskwaa River children ended up.

And that is what really linked the people of Miskwaa and Mozhay, their missing children. They who were schooled, ate, slept, punished, locked up, beaten, and abused, and who found each other and much more at institutions far away from home. My mother, Maggie LaForce, went to St. Veronique's in Canada, and my father, Andre Robineau, to the Harrod Indian School in Minnesota. Their children were John, me, and George. At Harrod, when Maggie was working as the matron's helper and Andre as a handyman, they both met Louis Gallette, a little boy with whom twenty years later Maggie would have two sons and my half-brothers, Vernon (Giizis) and Jerome (Buster; Biik) Gallette. Vernon disappeared in Italy during the Second World War without knowing that his girlfriend Dolly was expecting a baby, who Dolly named Vernon Gallette Jr. That baby, who his mother called Junior, was raised in Duluth and Dolly took the surname Gallette, which pleased Maggie and allowed Dolly the status of widowhood in the eyes of the landlord and the neighbors. Louis Gallette died shortly before his grandson Vernon Junior returned home to Duluth after his first enlistment in the Army. It was at Louis's funeral that Junior would see his cousin Loretta for the first time since she was a little girl.

Except for Louis's sister Lisette, I was the oldest person at his funeral, but not so old yet that I couldn't walk easily on my own to the coffin. One of Lisette's grandsons held out an arm for me to take; I shrugged it away.

"Can you see all right in here, Auntie?" he asked. I nodded.

When I was a girl some damage to my corneas had left me just about blinded to light. I can see fairly well if the lights in the room are dim or outside at twilight or on stormy days, but under electric or fluorescent lights, or outside in the sun, shards of brightness cut their way in zigzags across anything I try to look at. Dougherty's was my favorite place to go to funerals because the sconces on the walls were shaded by heavy amber glass, which cut the glare into just about nothing and was perfect for me. Approaching Louis's coffin, I looked down at what was left of the man who had been my mother's true love, both when they were together and when they were not, which was most of the time up to her death at the age of sixty. My mother, Maggie, who had lived for a good fifteen years past the Indian life expectancy at the time of her death, had looked so tired and worn; against the gray silk that lined the coffin and matched her hair she looked defeated. Louis, on the other hand, lasted a good twenty-five years past the Indian life expectancy and, for all his hard living and hard times, looked distinguished in his son Buster's sport coat, shirt, and tie; his face, an unlined bronze touched up by a little pink rouge on his sharp cheekbones, had an expression that was dignified and resolute.

I knelt on the padded bench in front of Louis's coffin, my knees and hips not much trouble at all yet in those days (although people were starting to act as if I could tip over and die at any moment—well, I didn't then and I am still around), and held my clasped hands in front of my chin. Perhaps I would pray, although of course Louis was gone; it was the fourth day, and his spirit would have reached the next world, and perhaps he was already with Maggie. As far as I could possibly know and have seen, he had been faithful to her and loved her truly, and he had earned the prayer.

"Bimosen, you must walk now, you who loved my mother. Bimosen noongoom, you must walk now, and don't look back; gawiin aabanaabi siin, gii gawbimin . . . ." My eyes dropped to Louis's fine-knuckled bronze hands that were arranged artistically on his chest, folded around a small crucifix. I pictured his walk through the travails of the four days and his arrival, Maggie grasping his hands in hers as she pulled him those last few steps from the cold of the river to the dryness of the shore.

The velvet padding shifted under my knees; next to me Dolly Gallette's bright yellow curls bobbed as she settled uneasily; as a Baptist she was not used to kneeling or to being that close to a crucifix. Vernon Junior stood behind his mother silently, then he shifted his weight from one foot to the other and cleared his throat. As I was about to rise and pat his arm—Louis was his grandfather, after all, even if he had seen him less than a dozen times, and Louis sober probably less than half of those—Vernon's eyes shifted to the side aisle of the viewing room, where a young woman walking toward the coffin had stopped about six feet back.

She stood there hesitantly, dressed in a yellow dotted-Swiss dress too summery for October, with her hands in the pockets of a light jacket that was too small. One hand left its pocket and smoothed, then brushed her hair away from that side of her face, exposing it to the room, yet it was not her face I recognized but her hair: dark brown, nearly black, with red highlights that caught and reflected light from the somber glow of the funeral hall sconces. I had seen that same color hair on Louis and on Lisette. It was Gallette hair, Miskwaa River hair, and the awkward girl with the round face who had walked into the intersecting histories of our lives and who Vernon Junior could not take his eyes off had to be one of the Gallette cousins.

Dolly recognized her right away.

ARTENSE

My cousin Loretta came to live with us for a while in Duluth the summer before we both started first grade. Although I had imagined us walking that block from our house to the St. Jean Baptiste School together every morning, holding hands and carrying our snacks for morning break, not long after Loretta arrived, her father, Albert Gallette, decided to move back up to Miskwaa River, past the far western edge of Mozhay Point Reservation, and took Loretta with him.

What I remember about that summer: getting things ready for Loretta; her arrival and how she looked at our house as though it was the most beautiful thing she had ever seen and she was the most fortunate girl in the world; and that she whispered to me in front of Junior that she loved him.

In the days leading up to Loretta's arrival my little sister Suzanne and I watched as our mother, Patsy, emptied a drawer in the dresser and then sorted through our clothes, even our underpants and socks, setting aside the largest for Loretta, who our mother said might not have extras, and who was just a little older and a little bigger than we were. Buster, my dad and Loretta's uncle, stacked our twin beds and brought in a single-size rollaway bed, borrowed from Patsy's dad's house. Suzanne could move to the rollaway, he said, and Loretta would have Suzanne's bed, which was now the lower bunk.

"Where will Betsy sleep?" Suzanne asked. Betsy was the cat, who slept on Suzanne's bed; she was weaving in and out of the legs of the bottom bunk, sniffing suspiciously at the clean sheets Patsy was tucking in mitered corners.

"With you . . . look." Patsy spread Suzanne's blanket on the rollaway and set Suzanne's turquoise plush stuffed puppy in the center. "Lay down, see what she does." The cat leaped onto the rollaway and settled against the stuffed toy. "See? I'll bet that's where she'll sleep."

"We'll have to be really nice to Loretta," Patsy told us. "She might be lonesome, and she'll have to get used to us."

As it turned out, Loretta was so used to staying at different houses that she got used to us, as Patsy would say, right away. At the same time, she didn't get used to us all, confused by Patsy's schedule of mealtimes and bath times, and mystified by Patsy's insistence on handwashing. When Buster brought her home after work the next day she got right out of the car and walked to the front door ahead of him, carrying a small wadded-up bundle of clothes that she held in two hands as he opened the door for her. She was dressed in a pair of denim overalls that were out at the knees and much too wide for her slight build, a limp white T-shirt, and broken-down buckled sandals; her thick dark red–brown hair, which I immediately envied because it reached to her waist, was bunched messily into a rubber band. She had the whitest teeth I had ever seen, with pointy, fang-like incisors and an eager smile. She looked, as Auntie Girlie would have said, full of beans and mischief.

"Say hello to your cousin Loretta," Buster said. "You remember Artense, and Suzanne, and here's Joseph, and Eveline." Loretta set the bundle of clothes on the floor. "Artense!" she said, took both of my hands, and began to jump up and down.

"Why don't you kids come in the kitchen and wash your hands for supper?" Patsy asked. "Artense, you can bring Loretta upstairs and show her the bunk beds and where she is going to put her things in the dresser, and you can wash your hands in the bathroom."

Loretta ran ahead of me, up the stairs, and then danced from room to room. In the bedroom she tossed her clothes onto the lower bunk, then kept the door open when she used the toilet and ignored me when I reminded her that we were supposed to wash our hands.

"Supper's ready; are you coming down?" Patsy called.

At the table Joseph watched, fascinated, by the speed with which Loretta ate her Spam and brown beans. She then ran a finger around her plate to pick up any leftover bean sauce, licked the sauce from her finger, and wiped her mouth on the bib of her overalls. "That was so good," she said.

Patsy, whose own mother had died when Patsy was three, mothered in a scenario set with what she had longed for in her own childhood and what she read in ladies' magazines and watched on the television that she and Buster had saved for and recently bought. Acting on both instinct and those acquired lessons she felt her way along, practicing, thinking, and then practicing again the accouterments of motherly consciousness and competence. Suzanne, Joseph, and I thought that Patsy could do anything. She sewed Halloween costumes, Red Riding Hood for me and a cotton Blue Fairy dress for Suzanne that she could also wear for everyday; at Thanksgiving she plucked the pinfeathers from a shockingly naked turkey and roasted and garnished it to look like a picture from her *Redbook* magazine; when Buster was at work she kept the furnace heating evenly, shoveling in coal with her strong, stringy arms; she carved a baby buggy figurine from a bar of Ivory soap and set it out as a decoration on the table in the bathroom, wrapping the leftover chips into a washcloth that she sewed all around and made into a soft scrubber for bath time. She had endless skills and talents, we thought, and when she applied some of those to Loretta we just regarded that as something she did and expected that she would, of course, succeed.

The first night Loretta spent in the lower bunk she slept in one of Patsy's nightgowns, shortened, a lacy pink rayon that Patsy said was the kind Queen Elizabeth wore to bed. Loretta stayed in that nightgown all the next day, twirling from time to time, which she explained was how Queen Elizabeth danced, while Patsy laundered her clothes in the wringer washer, turning the hand crank energetically for the overalls and gently for everything else. Patsy then hung everything on the clothesline in the backyard, commenting that it was a good drying day. We ate lunch and played princess in the dining room while we waited for Loretta's clothes to dry, then Patsy drew pictures of princesses and babies for us to color while she ironed Loretta's clothes. We let Loretta use the biggest, most whole crayons because she was still company; she pressed too hard and broke them. Eveline wept.

"Want to see what I'm doing with Loretta's overalls?" Patsy asked. "Not too close; the iron is hot." Patsy had cut two red iron-on patches into heart shapes, which she pressed over the knees of Loretta's overalls, which were in fact not knees at all but large holes. On the underside she had placed two pieces from the rag bag, which the hearts adhered to within the holes.

"Aren't these cute? They're Valentine pants!" said Patsy. She helped Loretta step into her clean, patched overalls and ironed T-shirt. For the rest of the day Loretta walked stiff-legged, in order to not bend the Valentines on her knees.

Valentine pants were just the kind of thing we had come to expect from our mother. Because Patsy could do anything, it never entered our heads that Loretta's first day at our house would be the best one, and that things would go downhill from there, and quickly.

DOLLY

I doubted that Patsy was calling me just to gab. Although she was on the phone all the time with her sisters and her girlfriends, she never called me, not that I expected it. After all, I was out working all day and she was home with her little kids, and she really kept herself busy, and I had just Junior at home and he was a big boy, going into junior high school that fall. So when Patsy called "just to gab," as she put it, I knew there had to be something she wanted to talk about, and so I waited through her running, worried conversation that was really with herself and not me: she and Buster were going to get school shoes for Artense and Suzanne, saddle shoes always looked nice if you kept the white leather clean; Buster had a lot of work lately and they were putting some money away for winter, you know how the house painting business is in January; did I hear that Donna LaForce had her baby up in Cloquet at the Indian Hospital, a boy; wasn't her shower fun? Then . . .

"Dolly, did you know that Albert's little girl, Loretta, has been here?"

"Yes, I heard that; how's that going?"

"He's taking her back; he told Buster they want her closer to Miskwaa River and so he's coming to get her tomorrow. She's going to stay with the Etiennes for the winter while Albert's at logging camp."

"Oh, the poor little thing, always getting moved around. I bet she'll miss your kids."

"They've been having fun, but if she's going to move to Miskwaa, it's just as well to take her there now, better sooner than later so she can start first grade and stay there for the whole year. I hope

Albert stays on the job all winter and doesn't move her again after she's settled."

"Settled for this time, you mean. Poor little thing."

"Ye-e-e-es . . . Look, you know Albert; you get along with him, don't you? How would you like to come here tomorrow for coffee? Buster's working and I don't even want to look at Albert if he shows up before Buster gets home."

"Sure, after lunch sometime, do you think? I'll bring some cookies for the kids."

The afternoon Loretta left for Mozhay Point was one of those hot September afternoons, just the right weather for the city truck to come through on Second Street, patching and tarring the beat-up blacktop. We could smell it from the bus stop, a block away from Patsy's.

Vernon Junior hadn't especially wanted to take the bus to Patsy and Buster's on the Saturday before school started, but he was a good boy and always willing to do just about anything I asked, and so although he probably would have liked to roam around with his friends when I told him Patsy needed some help, he didn't argue; in fact, he even offered to make a batch of brownies to bring along. Junior took pride in his cooking—he fixed supper just about every day and had it ready when I got home from work—and didn't use a mix for the brownies either, which he layered between sheets of waxed paper inside the shoebox that he carried from the bus stop to Patsy's house.

Little Joseph was sitting on the front stairs, holding a gray-striped cat that jumped from his lap and under the porch when it saw Junior. "Mama says to tell you to come in," he said politely and held the door.

Inside, the front hallway, which was scattered with the day's mail, a toy metal dump truck, a turquoise plush puppy, several picture books, a half-eaten egg salad sandwich, and what appeared to be dirty laundry, reeked of oil. In the middle of the hallway was a semi-cleared path into the living room where on a newspaper were a small pair of balled-up anklets and a pair of sandals streaked with tar, the source of the smell. Artense, holding Eveline, walked the floor between living and dining room, jiggling the infant, who was fussy. "Careful," she said, a pint-sized version of her father pointing with her lips toward the newspaper. "Don't step on the tar."

Patsy was nowhere to be seen. "Where's your mother?" I asked.

"She's busy washing Loretta," answered Suzanne. "We're supposed to be cleaning up this mess. Come on, Joseph; the clothes go in the basket, and the toys go in the toy box."

Patsy called from the back of the house, "Dolly? I'm in the kitchen!" Her voice was strained and breathy. "Watch out; there's tar on the linoleum."

On the white-painted doorway to the kitchen were several black smears of tar, about the height of where a little girl's hands would have reached, and on the floor several black streaks leading from the back door and as far into the dining room as Loretta had gotten when Patsy noticed.

Loretta and Patsy were at the kitchen sink, Patsy rubbing a bar of Ivory soap into a washcloth and Loretta, wearing only underpants, seated on the drain board with her feet in the sink. Next to her feet a green plaid play dress soaked in a dishpan of soapy water. "Almost done here," Patsy said and scrubbed at Loretta's knees.

"Eeek! A boy!" Loretta squealed. Junior quickly turned around, the shoebox of brownies in his hands.

"He didn't see anything—here, put these on." Patsy rinsed the washcloth and gave the little legs one more wipe-down, pulled a fresh blouse around Loretta, and lifted her to the floor, where she quickly pulled the clean Valentine overalls up over Loretta's small-boned body and buckled the shoulder straps. "You can wear Artense's shoes. It's hot out, you don't need socks."

Loretta pulled the baggy legs of her overalls wide and curtseyed. "This is how the queen does it," she said to Junior. "Now, you bow."

"Hand her majesty the brownies, why don't you, Junior?" I directed.

Patsy, squeezing rinse water out of the dress and then rinsing the dishpan, set it upside down on the drain board with enough force that it clattered. "I'll make some coffee," she said. "Albert should be here pretty soon." She looked exhausted, just worn out.

"I'll do it," I said. "Here, Junior, why don't you give each of the kids a brownie—have them sit at the dining room table—and then maybe you can take Loretta and Artense out for a walk around the block. Would you girls like to go for a walk around the block with Junior? When you get back you can tidy up the house a little. Here, Patsy; you just sit and take a load off. I'll take care of this."

Patsy, who ordinarily would have insisted that she do it all herself, dried her hands on a dish towel, then sat and watched me and Junior get the kids settled, before Junior headed out the back door with Artense and Loretta. Then Patsy set her coffee cup into its saucer and told me about her week with Loretta—whose fault it *wasn't* that she, Patsy, could not get the poor little thing aligned with Patsy's efforts to run a calm, orderly household that produced children who would be clean, well-behaved, and smart in school, children who would have and be all that she and Buster dreamed for them.

"It's not her fault," she repeated. "It's mine, and I think Buster knew how glad I am that she's leaving."

What I told her was not just to make her feel better; it was also the truth. There was only so much a person could do, I told her, only so far one person could stretch. Albert had his troubles, but he would always have troubles, and Patsy was right, it wasn't Loretta's fault. But neither was it Patsy's. She was just one person, just one human being, like everybody else. Like me.

"You've done what you could," I said. "Look what nice shape her clothes are in now, and how cute she looks with her bangs trimmed. Don't you feel bad, and don't you worry about anything."

Patsy took a sip of water and grimaced.

"She'll be fine," I continued, not certain about that but wanting to buck Patsy up. "And this way she can see Albert when he's done with logging season."

Patsy looked thoughtfully at the ceiling, swallowed twice, said "I'll be right back," and ran upstairs to the bathroom, where she threw up. I didn't ask if she was expecting again.

ARTENSE

Dolly had given Junior a nickel and told him to take me and Loretta down to Crawford's, the corner store, for penny candy for each of us and enough to bring back for Suzanne and Joseph ("Don't get hard candy for the little kids; I don't want anybody choking to death," she had ordered). In back of the glassed-in candy counter Mrs. Crawford, bent almost double with her head inside the sliding doors, pressed her hand into the small of her aching back as she hovered over the displays, left to right from Chum Gum to chocolate babies to candy dots to peppermint sticks, fishing out our selections and telling us that once she touched a piece it was ours, no changing, so make sure you have your mind made up.

We left with the candy in a brown paper sack: a rainbow strip of candy dots each for me and Loretta; orange slices for Suzanne and Joseph, and two twists of red licorice for Vernon Junior. Outside, the tar truck had parked and three men were taking a break, drinking coffee from their thermos mugs. Junior told us to wait on the sidewalk for a minute and not to move, he'd be right back. He walked up to the men and spoke to the man who was leaning on a shovel, who reached into the bed of the truck and handed Junior a small wad of tar.

"Let's go back," Junior said to us. "Thanks," he called back to the man with the shovel, who lifted one hand in a half-wave.

"What are you going to do with that?" I asked.

"Chew it like gum; see?" He popped it into his mouth; horrified, I stared. "I didn't have to spend money on gum, so I bought licorice, and I still have something to chew. And it makes nice snoose." He spat a little stream to the side, into the grass. "Don't tell my ma."

"Can I carry the bag of candy?" I didn't want Patsy or Dolly to see tar on the bag.

Junior held the bag out in my direction, and as I reached for it Loretta said, "I want to!" and grabbed it out of my hand. I grabbed it back, and Junior took the bag out of my hand and held it over our heads. Loretta leaped, knocking the bag out of Junior's grip; the bag sailed onto the grass and landed upright, with the neat double-fold crimped by Mrs. Crawford across the top intact. Loretta was not as fortunate; she stumbled, falling to her hands and knees. Sitting up she swiped at her nose with one hand, looked down, and cried, "Ow, ow, ow, I'm bleeding! Where's the candy?"

I picked up the bag, which still looked clean with no sign of blood or tar, thank goodness. Junior helped Loretta to stand.

"Your nose isn't bleeding much," he said. "Are you bleeding anyplace else?"

The heels of Loretta's hands were raw where the concrete had scraped the skin off and speckled with grit from the sidewalk; one of the Valentine heart patches on her knees had held up, the other had torn from the fabric and hung loose, exposing her other knee, which was as raw-looking as her hands.

"I think you're gonna live," said Vernon. "Want me to carry you?" Loretta snuffled and nodded her head, and he picked her up with one arm behind her knees and the other around her shoulders.

Loretta snuffled again and then buried her face in Vernon's shirt. "I don't want to go to Miskwaa," she mumbled wetly. "I want to stay here with Artense."

Junior jiggled Loretta the way I did Eveline when she was fussing. "It's nice up there," he said, a twelve-year-old boy soothing our fanciful bleeding little cousin as he wiped away her tears and bloody, running nose with his bare hand. "My dad lived at Mozhay Point when he was a little boy; he was at Miskwaa a lot of times."

"Where does he live now?"

"He died before I was born. I've been up there, though, to Mozhay and to Miskwaa, too, fishing. We'll come up to see you sometime."

"Will you bring Artense?"

"Sure, Artense can come."

"I'll give you your shoes back when you come," Loretta said to me. "And we can all go fishing together."

"Whatever you say, Queen Loretta," said Junior.

"My prince," she said to Junior.

"I love him," she whispered to me.

DOLLY

Auntie Girlie recognized Loretta before I did. It had been years since I had seen her, and she had grown from that ragamuffin of a little girl into the sad, awkward young woman who showed up by herself to Louis Gallette's funeral.

"Was that Loretta Gallette?" Girlie whispered to me. Junior listened, and I imagined Girlie's breath bearing Loretta's name settling on his hands and arms like an anointing.

"P.G.?" I mouthed at Girlie, raising my eyebrows and shoulders.

Girlie pursed her lips around a little round O in that way the Robineau women had.

She must be in her late teens, I thought. Loretta hadn't had a figure or that axle-grease eyeliner last time I saw her when she was still a scruffy-looking little thing, what, three or four years ago? Probably in late summer after Junior graduated from high school, not long after he left for basic training. If I am remembering it correctly, Louis's niece Babe had some visitors from Miskwaa, some of the Gallettes who were visiting around Duluth, staying at various people's houses until their welcome wore out. They had some of the Dommages along, too, must have been a car packed full of people for the trip, seven or eight including Annie Dommage, who had brought along her little niece Loretta, who was Albert Gallette's daughter. I don't know if Albert was married to Frances Dommage when Loretta was born; I am fairly certain that he wasn't around at the time, but Frances had the hospital fill in his name on the baby girl's birth certificate and named her Loretta Marie Gallette. Frances was a drinker, a bad alcoholic, and Loretta was raised by the Gallettes at Miskwaa, whoever was able to take her, and so she was moved from household to household.

My situation could have been like Loretta's if it wasn't for Maggie Robineau, whose son is the father of my boy, Vernon Gallette Jr. I met Vernon—Senior, that is—in Minneapolis, where I was living with my mother and working the mangle at a laundry right near the end of the Second World War. He and his cousin Sam Sweet were working as pin boys at the Palace Bowl, where a girlfriend and I were on a double date with some young fellows whose names I have forgotten.

Vernon. My goodness, he was so good-looking, with a nice smile and this way of ducking his head when he talked, and easy-going? Well, he had to be the easiest-going boy in the world, and dying to go into the service like his older brothers—his mother gave her signed permission for him to enlist, which he did right after his seventeenth birthday. We had a party for him at the Palace Bowl along with the other pin boys, and the boss Mr. Mountbatten, and

Ingrum who worked there, and Ingrum's lady love, Winifred. Now Mother wasn't too crazy about my having this Indian boyfriend, but she would have come to the party, glad to see him leave, except for her job at the flour mill, where she worked second shift. Still, she sent her wishes for good luck—if she had known that I was thinking that I might be expecting at the time, I don't know what she would have done about the party, or about anything else.

So, I was P.G., "a girl in trouble," as they said in those days. The circumstances—oh my, there have been other girls in my situation—eighteen years old and unmarried, expecting a baby and not wanting to tell the father. I first suspected before Vernon left, and there was no point in causing him worry. Thinking about telling Mother made me feel sick, and then things got worse: Vernon went missing in action somewhere in Italy (as far as we were ever able to tell), and we never saw or heard from him again. The news went to Vernon's mother, Maggie, who wrote a postcard to his cousin Sam. When Sam told me and let me read the postcard, I felt like I had known it all along, isn't that funny?

The only person who had known I even had a suspicion I was pregnant was Winnie, Ingrum's girlfriend at the Palace. Now, because Winnie and Ingrum are long dead, and because I know you won't go gossiping this to everybody you know, and because it was such a long time ago, I will tell you this: Winnie was, in fact, a man. Now, she was a real ladylike lady, gracious and so high-class except that she wore such heavy pancake makeup, and she was doted on by Ingrum. They were unable to tell this to anyone, of course, because of how things were during those times; certainly, they could not marry and so were living in sin, which was a big bad deal in those days, too. Their life together must have been unimaginably difficult, yet they never seemed to quarrel or appear unhappy with one another; they kept up a flirtatious, funny conversation, like sweethearts who had a little secret, which was certainly so and then some, and a cheery attitude with themselves and everyone around them. Married or not, man and wife or not, they were the most devoted couple I ever knew, and Winnie was a wonderful woman, a lady of great sentiment and generosity. And so nice to Vernon and Sam, and especially to me. I confided in her not long after Vernon left and she was kindness itself.

Once I was two months gone and really sure, Winnie thought I should write to Mother. "Why, a baby is God's greatest blessing," she said. "Ingrum and I would have loved children, but God has His reasons for everything."

I reminded her of how Mother felt about Vernon. "How can I do that? I can't even think what she'll do, can you?" I asked as we watched Ingrum bowl. "How long can I even work? They're not going to let me stay at the laundry once I'm showing. What will Mother do without my paycheck?"

Winnie always looked at things through rose-colored glasses. "Your mother is your best friend," she answered. She blew a smoke ring and then two more, three perfect Os that floated over the scoring table and disappeared. "You'll see," she said and patted my hand. "Besides, what did she do without your paycheck before you left school? You haven't been working for even a year."

When I told her, Mother cried for almost two days, missing work and pay, and then she threw me out. I didn't hold it against her; she certainly had her own troubles.

Winnie felt really terrible that she had been wrong about Mother, but she assured me that Mother would come around in her thinking eventually. She offered to let me stay with her in the boarding house (she and Ingrum as an unmarried couple rented separate rooms, of course; this was the 1940s). The landlady told her that would be all right for a while, and that I could sleep on the guest cot for free because of the circumstances, but not permanently. Once the baby was born, I would have to rent my own room if I wanted to stay.

"Well, that's settled!" said Winnie. "And won't it be fun to have a baby around! Don't you worry about a thing, sweetheart; why, one of these days maybe we can even rent a house and we'll all be together, one big happy family—and once your mama sees her grandchild, she'll come around, wait and see. Are you hoping for a girl or a boy?"

When Winnie said that, I started to realize that not only was I expecting and in big trouble, but that the end result was going to be a new person, a baby I would have to take care of beyond just finding a place to sleep. How long did I have before I started to show? Where would I get money for a doctor, the hospital, rent, and somebody to watch the baby while I worked? Thrilled though Winnie was about the prospect, and willing though Ingrum was to keep her happy, I couldn't take their help indefinitely, and, I am a little ashamed to say, I wanted something better in life than the boarding house, the Palace Bowl, and being swallowed up by two people who couldn't have their own children.

Vernon had talked about his mother sometimes, about their house in Duluth and their relatives and friends there, and at the Mozhay Point Reservation. Listening to his stories about people visiting at their house, it seemed to me that Maggie helped a lot of people out. Would she help me, the mother of Vernon's baby?

Not wanting to hurt her feelings, I told Winnie that Maggie had written to me and said that I would be welcome at her house, that she wanted to help with her grandchild, doing my best to sound like I wasn't making this up. Winnie thought this was the best news she had ever heard, said she would miss me, but that she and Ingrum wished me all the best. A week later she and Ingrum walked with me to the bus depot where they bought me a one-way ticket to Duluth— Winnie a little tearful as she pressed a flat gift-wrapped box into my hand and Ingrum's voice a tremolo as he gave me a bank envelope from Mr. Mountbatten, the owner at the Palace Bowl.

"If you need anything you call us at the Palace—call collect and reverse the charges," he said. "And don't forget to write."

I promised I would write often and boarded, taking a window seat. The last thing I saw as the bus pulled out was Winnie and Ingrum standing right underneath my window, arm in arm and smiling. Ingrum was waving, his Adam's apple bobbing sadly up and down, and Winnie dabbed at her eyes with one of her lacy handkerchiefs.

During most of the six-hour trip to Duluth, I pretended that Vernon was sitting on the seat next to me and kept up a running conversation in my mind with him about our new life in Duluth. He thought that we would stay with his mother until we were on our feet. "Oh, you're going to like her," he said, "and she is going to be crazy about you. Wait till she hears we're getting married!" I imagined that she wouldn't mind when I started to show, that she might even guess about the baby before that, and then thinking about his mother brought me back to what was real—Vernon missing in Italy and me on my way to surprise Maggie. I wondered what she would say when I showed up at her door, gripping Winnie's valise full of my clothes, and pregnant. I would have to tell her about the baby right away, which reminded me of the gift-wrapped box. I opened it carefully in order to save the paper, printed with pink and blue bunnies, for a souvenir. Inside was a white machine-knit baby sweater with a matching bonnet and booties, both trimmed with white ribbon. In the envelope were five ten-dollar bills and a note: *Best of luck and best wishes from your friends at the Palace Bowl. Sincerely, Montie.* I rewrapped the baby gift, tucking the money inside the hat, and opened Winnie's valise. As I tucked the box down the side I saw that Winnie had set on top of my clothes a brand-new box of Blondine, the hair lightener we both liked. They don't make Blondine anymore and haven't in years, but I still keep my hair that color and in curls, like Winnie's.

Maggie took me in, just like that, and figured out that I was expecting without my even telling her. I stayed in the house almost all the time, too sad to go out, but I helped with housework and cooking, and even with never leaving the backyard, I got to know more people than I ever had before in my life. Six months later my baby, Vernon Junior, was born in Maggie's bedroom, delivered by Maggie and her sister Helen, who had chased everyone from the house out of consideration for me. When Junior had been bathed and was placed in my arms, wrapped in a tiny patchwork quilt made by Helen, I stared and he stared back; I swear he smiled just like Vernon. He looked so much like his father that I could hardly take my eyes off him, but I handed him to Maggie, who cupped one hand over his head, stroking his fine black hair. Helen caressed his feet, feeling for them through the quilt, and wept.

Maggie and I wrote to my mother and mailed our letters in the same envelope, mine telling her about the baby and Maggie's inviting her to come for a visit. My mother wrote back to say that she would be up soon, probably near the end of the month and would stay for a couple of days if that would be all right. She never made it, however; two weeks later we received a telegram from her boss informing us of her death, from a heart attack at work. I still tear up thinking about that; how sad it was that we lost each other twice and that she never got to see Vernon Junior, the most beautiful baby ever born.

Winnie and Ingrum took the bus up from Minneapolis for Junior's baptism, which in honor of Maggie's being Catholic, took place at St. Clement's. This pleased Winnie, too, who was a devout Catholic, and the priest never knew that Vernon Jr.'s godparents were not a married couple. Or anything else. All he asked was if they had both been baptized Catholic — which they both were — at which parish, and if they were practicing Catholics. Which they both were, if the word *practicing* was applied in a different sense to each. The priest's questions actually gave me the heebie-jeebies a little, since Winnie and Ingrum also promised that they would oversee Baby Vernon's spiritual life and make sure he was raised in "the Church," but I did it for Maggie and saw that he made his First Communion and was confirmed. After all, Winnie and Ingrum had promised. And renounced Satan for him, too, right there at the baptismal font.

We stayed at Maggie's house for a few years, Junior and I, while I got on my feet. At first I got a job at a laundry just a few blocks away from the house, but then Maggie got me on at the mattress factory and I earned my living sewing—eventually moving on to canvas tents and awnings, work that was hard on the hands but paid well—and cleaning houses. I learned all kinds of things from Maggie, like some of the LaForce family stories as well as the Gallettes', and I learned to talk a little Indian, not much but enough that the old people in the family were happy about it and pleased to see that Junior was being raised properly. When Maggie died—too young—I had some money that she had made sure I saved and was able to rent my own place, a two-bedroom house that eventually the landlord's son sold to me on a contract for deed. I have lived there ever since.

Vernon Junior was, as I said, the most beautiful baby ever born, and I have the pictures to prove it. He grew to be a lot huskier than his father but had the same big, open-mouthed smile that creased his cheeks, and those same almond-shaped brown eyes that looked as though he was about to laugh, even if he wasn't. He was a quiet boy, close to his friend Howard Dulebohn who was quiet, too, and it was through Howard that Junior began singing with Noel Dulebohn, Beryl's husband, on the Sweetgrass drum when the men visited from Mozhay.

Right after high school Junior enlisted in the Army, and at the end of his first enlistment thought he might like to be career army, so he re-upped. Over the years he traveled all over the world, getting stationed in Germany, Hawaii, and one year somewhere in Africa; he sent me souvenirs from those places and he did end up doing two tours in Vietnam, which left him a little nervous. In fact, in the line of work he was in, communications, he regularly volunteered for night duty, which he found easier to take than the daylight. Once he had his twenty years in, he retired and came home, to live in our own little house and help out. As you can probably imagine, this was a mother's dream.

A mother doesn't expect to have her son to herself all her life; I expected and even hoped that while he was in the service he would meet some nice young woman and get married. I would have grandchildren, and they would come to visit every year until he retired, when they would all move to Duluth, or they would invite me to come live wherever they decided to settle. It turned out that my imagining all this was like something Winnie would have done.

It just happened that Junior was home on leave when his grandfather Louis Gallette died. We went to the funeral, which was held at Dougherty's Funeral Home, and I was so proud for everybody to see Junior because he was so big and strong, so tanned and good-looking. A Catholic priest came to do the service, which was not a Mass I was relieved to see, as I never could get used to that kind of religion. Not that I have anything against it—Junior still goes sometimes himself. We did, however, have to go up and kneel on this fancy carved piece of furniture that looked like something out of a medieval castle or else that Vatican where the Pope of Rome lives, a little velvet-padded bench with a shelf to rest your arms on when you prayed over the coffin, two people at a time. Angeline Robineau, Maggie's oldest daughter who she called Girlie, was already on one side of that fancy kneeler, hunched over praying like she was some of kind of nun and dangling this beadwork bracelet over the corpse, finally tucking it into Louis's breast pocket and fanning it out so it would look nice, I guess. Junior waited behind me as I knelt next to her and looked down at Louis; they had done a nice job on him and he was wearing Buster's sport coat and a tie; I had never seen him looking so spiffed up. I prayed for Jesus to take Louis into his loving arms and fly him to Heaven (no point in asking for flocks of angels, as I didn't want to push it, given the life Louis had led) and then turned to Junior; I was going to give him my half of the kneeler since it looked like Girlie was going to be there a while. That's when I noticed this girl who was standing behind Girlie, on the side opposite of Junior.

She had to be one of the Gallettes; she looked just like them, with that slight build and that hair, so dark it was almost black and with those red highlights, the same color as Junior's. My guess was that she was from that bunch still living at Miskwaa, and I remembered well how often they and the Dommages, one of the other Miskwaa families that they had married into too often, showed up at Maggie's house and mooched off her. Half the time they left at the end of their visits with something she felt compelled to give them: coats, blankets, food, once even her couch. They never had a pot to pee in and seemed to have no idea at all how to get one by honest work. It was really their luckiest day when Maggie went to work at the Indian boarding school over at Harrod—that was where most of the Gallette children from Miskwaa had been sent, including Louis Gallette and his sister Lisette, and that is where Louis first saw Maggie. How they ended up together years after I don't really know. The fact is that Maggie had been married to Andre Robineau for a good ten years when Louis came into the picture, and her last two children, Vernon and Buster, were Louis's. I am not faulting Maggie; goodness knows Andre was terrible to her and Louis sweet, though rarely around for the boys, as Vernon told me. However, once Louis arrived in the picture, it was inevitable that Maggie would have to take on the entire Gallette family, and there were a lot of them, with their issues and their problems. They came and went, and so did Maggie's troubles.

I thought all that within two seconds as I looked over that girl. Nobody had thought much about if any of the Miskwaa Gallettes might show up at Louis's funeral: ever broke, they would not have had the gas money, and in the shock and confusion over Louis's unexpected death I don't think anyone would have thought to offer them money or a place to stay. This girl, though, must have already been living in Duluth and either was hoping that she might get a good meal or was there to pay respects on behalf of the family—more likely the first, in my opinion. She certainly looked alone, and cold in that light summer dress and short jacket on that chilly day. With her arms crossed and folded across her stomach—I knew that look. Pregnant, I would have bet, and of course not married, so she was in trouble. I was about to speak to her, to say hello, when I saw that Junior was looking at her. Junior, who had never even had a serious girlfriend, was looking at this little scrap of yellow sundress, red-black hair, and goose-pimpled bare legs—did he notice her pot belly, and that her coat was pulled so tightly across her front that it rode up above her behind in the back?—as though he was ready to feed her, warm her, and take her away to care for her for the rest of their days.

The Gallette girl only glanced at Junior as she took her place on the kneeler next to Girlie. I thanked the Lord that my boy was on the side where he could see the unmarked side of her face; on the other, the faint gray shadow of a week-old black eye and the slight puffiness of a fist's impact showed on the girl's lip. If Junior had been standing on her other side he might have decided to rescue her then and there, and believe me, there is no way to pull a Gallette out of the quicksand that has deepened over the past century; that whole bunch at Miskwaa would only pull you right in and you'd never get out. I know it's not their fault, but it's not mine, either, and it is especially not Junior's.

In the next minute the priest walked into the room and everyone stood. Junior, Girlie, and I took the nearest chairs, and the girl slipped to the back of the room.

"Was that Loretta Gallette?" Girlie whispered to me. Junior listened.

"The Lord be with you," intoned the priest.

"And with your spirit," I joined in with the Catholics.

Loretta must have left Dougherty's right at the end of the service; she was nowhere to be seen, though I could see Junior looking around.

I am not proud of what I did next, but it was for the best, really. Much as I admired Maggie's generosity with Louis's family and everybody else, I simply was not born with the same spirit, and perhaps I was a little jealous in my guarding of my son's attention. If I were a different kind of person, someone like Maggie, say, I might have let things run their course; if I were someone like Winnie, I would have joyfully, sentimentally grabbed the moment and made the most of the miracle. Instead I said to Junior, "Can you find Auntie Girlie and help her into the car? I promised her a ride."

My unsaid words were "Take your mind off Loretta: you're related to her, she's too young for you, and she looks like a pack of trouble." Nipped that right in the bud, I thought at the time. Distracted by the search for Girlie, who I had seen shuffling with Artense to the ladies' room, swatting a couple of times at Artense's offered arm, Junior hung around to await their emergence through the ladies' room door. Still on her feet but tiring, Girlie leaned droopily onto Artense's shoulder and allowed Junior to take her purse, which he held awkwardly. At the curb, occupied by the gymnastics required by both Junior and Artense to hold Girlie's long, ungainly body upright and balanced in spite of her determination to shrug away their hands, and then fitted like a jigsaw puzzle piece through the car door and into the back seat, Junior's attention was averted from seeing what I saw, which was Loretta exiting the church by the side door, all by herself. At Babe's house, where everybody was heading for some food, he and Artense would have to unwind Girlie from the car and then up the front steps and onto Babe's most comfortable easy chair. I would keep him waiting on the old lady and he wouldn't have time to do much else; if Girlie got the two or three little glasses of Dubonnet she liked into her, Junior would be even busier listening to her tell him about when she learned to play the organ at the Harrod Indian school and who knows what else.

When his leave was over, Junior would be going overseas again and would forget all about Loretta, who couldn't help it that she was a pack of trouble, and neither could I. Besides, they were cousins—not first cousins, but with the Gallettes you never can tell, God knows.

Don't try telling me you wouldn't have done the same.

Mesabi

AZURE SKY

I don't remember much from the first couple of years after Loretta left us at the County, except that Rain wasn't there. Any memories I have aren't in color, just a dusky, hazy gray: a bed in a lower bunk and meals at a long Formica table, a man in green janitor's clothes bringing me a booster seat; watching cartoons on television in a hot basement room; a three-quarters moon shining through the window of an acrid-smelling bathroom, its light leaving patterns on the pebbled vinyl floor; kneeling on a kitchen chair over a sink where an elderly woman gently washed my hair. And looking first for Rainy at each new place I moved.

Loretta had told the social worker that she was going to the hospital for a while and would come get us when she got out. But she never showed up. During those dusty and hazy early years I occasionally asked where she was, and the answer was always a diversion: time to wash your hands for lunch, let's see what's on TV. I began to wonder if she had died, or forgotten us, even if she had other children, and if she did, what their names might be.

I still wonder.

In that twilight fog of loneliness I imagined for myself a brother—at least that is what everybody told me when I talked about him, that he was my imaginary friend. Who was I to argue with them? But I knew he was real.

My big brother's name was Hussley, and we met at the front doors of the Northwoods Children's home. Hussley had dark red hair and freckles and wore a striped T-shirt under a pair of denim bib overalls. He stood next to my chair when I ate, he sat next to me on the couch in the rec room. At night he lay on the floor next to my bed, awake all night, keeping watch.

That the adults around me couldn't see Hussley didn't make him any less real, and his existence made them feel sorry for me while at the same time unnerving them.

"I'll share my mashed potatoes with Hussley," I told one of the kitchen ladies at Northwoods.

"Who's Hussley?" she asked, looking around.

"Right here. Do you want some?" I asked what the kitchen lady saw as an empty space next to me on the bench.

"Is he your imaginary friend?"

"He's my brother."

"Oh, sweetheart, would he like his own little dish of Jell-O?" she asked tearfully.

One evening, Hussley came dangerously close to being smothered by the janitor in the rec room. As we were waiting for the Scooby-Doo show on TV, the three-to-eleven shift worker Miss Peggy settled the little kids, that would be me and my friends LaTasha and Brittany, on the couch. I left room at the end for Hussley, who liked Scooby-Doo because he could almost talk. The janitor, skinny old Mr. Lyle, decided to watch Scooby too, and thinking there was a space open on the couch, he walked right over and sat.

"Mr. Lyle, you're sitting on Hussley!"

The janitor jumped up from the couch; I had never seen him

move so fast. Then he looked confused. "Who did I sit on?" he asked.

I checked to make sure that Hussley was all right. "He's the boy sitting right *there*," I said.

"Oh." Mr. Lyle looked at the couch cushion and then at me. "Hussley." He half-laughed nervously and moved to a chair.

A few years later, when Rain and I went to live at Sherry's, Hussley disappeared. I haven't seen him since, but it comforts me to think that he is still here, unseen.

It was because Sherry was willing to take two sisters that Rain and I saw each other again, and although our new foster home would be in the town of Mesabi, up north on the Iron Range and a long way from Duluth, I didn't worry at all about leaving Northwoods because I would see my sister again and we would live in a real house, with a family.

When I got out of the social worker's car, Rain was standing in the front yard, waving her arm back and forth as far as she could stretch so that we could see her and not drive past the house. At first she didn't look like herself; I paused to give her a good look and realized that she was doing the same to me. Then we stood side by side, our shoulders and arms and hips pressed tightly, to face our new world together.

"Where were you, Azure?" my sister asked. "I was looking for you for a long time."

I told her that I had been in Duluth, and described Northwoods: the other girls in the dormitory, the meals, the activity room in the basement. There was no point in telling her about anything before that, especially the moonlit bathroom curtains and floor in the house I lived in before Northwoods.

"Did you live with nice people?" I asked my sister.

She never did answer.

· · ·

We stayed with Sherry, her husband Don, and their two little boys, Andrew and Erik, for three years. When Rain was ten and I almost nine—and long after Sherry couldn't take it anymore—the County moved us to Mrs. Kukonen's house out in the townships.

Sherry was what Mrs. Kukonen would call a nervous wreck. She cried a lot but I couldn't blame her. We were a lot of work, and it was clear from listening to her and Don argue, which they did a lot, that the reason she had taken us in was to try to bring in some money, because everybody else's wives worked and helped out, and why couldn't she? When we first got there, she would ask Don for a hand around the house or with the kids every so often; he always had something else to do. This led to fights, with Don finally telling her that what she brought in from the County barely covered what it cost to have us there, and when she pulled her own weight with the money around here, *then* she could whine about the housework.

"Take it or leave it, Sherry; you can get a job or you can stay home, your choice. I don't want to hear about it anymore."

I felt sorry for Sherry, and I learned that even though she cried a lot, she could also take a lot. And she was always nice to Rain and me—as nice as she was to Andrew and Erik, her own boys. The five of us went everywhere together on the days Sherry needed the car for errands. On those days we'd get up early in the morning, bring Don to work, then run errands: we went to the bank, to the grocery store, to her sister Bev's house for coffee, to the library, to the WIC meeting for playtime while the mothers listened to the County nurse talk about nutrition and then to pick up the coupons for milk, cheese, cereal, and produce. Our favorite, though, was the Salvation Army store: on Salvation Army days we watched the boys and went through the toy bins while Sherry picked through the kids' clothes and tried on clothes for herself. Sherry was a fussy shopper, inspecting every inch of seams, pulling at armpits for signs of weakness, laying a boy's jacket across a table to go over the lining and work the zipper up and down. We never left empty-handed, and usually there was something for each of us. On the best day of all, as we were lining up at the counter to pay, Sherry noticed a shoebox on the floor next to a stack of clothing waiting to be priced. From one end of the broken and torn box top a pair of doll's legs with impossibly tiny feet stuck straight out.

"Are those Barbie dolls in there? Can I look?" she asked.

Inside were a half-dozen naked Barbie dolls lying on a layer of tiny clothes and plastic high heels. Barbies! My heart pounded.

"They're not very clean—their hair is all tangled, and the whole box kind of stinks," Sherry commented. My heart sank. Sherry sniffed at the box again. "Would you take a dollar?"

The Salvation Army lady said she could.

Rain and I took turns holding the shoebox in the car. At the house Sherry dumped the whole box into the kitchen sink and washed everything in dish detergent, then lay the dolls and clothes out on a bath towel to dry. She untangled the Barbies' hair carefully with her own wide-toothed comb and trimmed off the mats. Then she went into her sock drawer and took out a handful of socks that were missing mates, cut off the toes, and made slits at the side.

"This is how you make your own Barbie clothes," she said. "Aren't they cute?"

With the tops rolled down to off-the-shoulder height they were more than cute, especially the lacy knee sock that had been missing its mate but was too pretty to toss.

We learned to cook by helping Sherry, who made the best meals I have ever eaten. How she did this I don't know, but she had a repertoire of a half-dozen "success meals," as she called them, most based on canned goods. Little that she bought was fresh, and she used minimal flavorings or spices. She and her husband argued during most of the meals, at least when he wasn't chewing and swallowing, and yet I cannot remember a meal that wasn't delicious. Sherry taught me how to cook, and although I don't have the

magic touch she must have been born with, I can—like Sherry—
make a good meal from just about anything.

This came about because of these terrific headaches that Sherry
got sometimes. It was on an afternoon that she had taken four Ex-
cedrin pills and was stumbling around the kitchen that I asked if I
could help. She looked so surprised—it might have been the first
offer of help she had ever had. "Sure; here, you can open a can of
brown beans, and a can of corn, two cans of those little potatoes, and
put them in saucepans on the stove—turn the knobs to medium."
Sherry took a dishcloth from the drawer, wetted it at the sink, and sat
at the kitchen table pressing the cloth lightly to her forehead as she
watched me. "Can you stack eight slices of bread on a plate, too, and
get out the margarine? Put them all on the table with silverware?"

"Can I help, too?" Rain and the boys asked. Sherry told Rain
that she could help the next day, and in the meantime, she would
be in charge of clearing off the dining room table and setting up the
silverware and glasses.

"Can we cook, too?" Andrew and Erik looked ready to tear up
the kitchen. "We'll make brownies!"

The dish towel had slipped down Sherry's forehead to her eye-
lashes; she blinked slowly, peering out like a heavy-lidded tortoise.
"You can help by sitting on the couch."

"The couuuuch," the boys whined. "We want to heeeeeee-elp."

"If you stay on that couch and I don't hear a peep out of you
until your dad gets home, I'll pay you a quarter. Each. Starting this
second." The boys trotted out of the room, and the tortoise pulled
the wet dish towel back down over her eyelids.

By the time Don got home Sherry was feeling better, and after he had washed up and roughed around with the boys, she and
I filled plates from the stove, arranging canned potatoes, beans,
and corn in neat mounds that didn't touch. We carried the plates
into the dining room and placed them in front of Don, Rain, and
the boys, Don's expression becoming somewhat suspicious when

Sherry announced that Azure had cooked the whole dinner. Erik inhaled the steam rising from his plate and said, "Smells good," then we all dug right in and ate with the same appetite we had during all of Sherry's delectable meals.

Sherry said I had been a big help and next put me to work on the grocery list. This meant that every week we discussed how many cans of brown beans were needed, and how many of green beans and corn, or if we were low on Spam, or canned cream soup, or egg noodles, or brownie mix. I began to love our skinny, harried foster mother, and without telling Rain, I would imagine sometimes that Sherry would adopt us and become our official mother.

I knew that it was just pretend, because if she had begun to love us back and want to adopt us, wouldn't she have called us by our correct names? She called her little boys, her own children Andrew and Erik and never mixed them up like she did me and Rain. Sometimes she called me and Rain by each other's names when she got distracted, which was understandable, I told myself; after all, although I was younger than Rainy, she was so much smaller, and although she was the older sister she talked like a baby. I told myself that it was no wonder Sherry got mixed up—all the time aware she never got Andrew and Erik mixed up, even though they looked almost like twins.

And, really, why would Sherry want to adopt me and Rain when she was always stressed about money and Don was always on her about it? There was hardly anything left over after food and clothes for those girls, he said; they never got to go out because the babysitter charged too much, and who wants to watch four kids, anyway? If we wanted more kids—which we don't—we would have our own, Don said. If Sherry wanted to save some money, she should just quit smoking, Don said. But don't go eating up whatever you save just because you quit smoking, he said; don't be one of those women who get fat, he said. Then he put his mouth right by her ear and reached across her back and under her arm to place a hand on her breast. "Except right here," he said, and because the boys and Rain were wrestling around on the floor and laughing—which they would do until somebody decided they were hurt and would cry—he didn't notice that I was listening over the racket.

Don breathed onto Sherry's ear and the side of her neck. "And if you wanted little Indians maybe you should have married one," he half-whispered, squeezing her breast. "Like Michael Washington; I bet that girlfriend of his would have pounded the snot out of you if she ever found out." Sherry pushed Don's arm away and walked out of the room.

After Sherry quit smoking to try to cut expenses, things got worse. She went on a diet of cheese, apples, milk, and Ry-Krisp but gained five pounds; she cut out cheese and chewed ice cubes when she got too hungry but became a little light-headed and mixed up in the afternoons and so took to calling both of us Azure-Rain, to save on confusion.

The boys, who were toddlers when we moved in, knew us as half of that single entity, Azure-Rain—which is what they learned to call either one of us when they learned to talk.

"No, Azure-Rain," the smaller boy, Erik, giggled at me when I sat my Barbie doll in the back of his Tonka truck for a ride. "That's a boy toy." I made a revving noise, careening the truck around the couch toward Rainy's feet, causing the boys to laugh uncontrollably.

"Look out, Azure-Rain, Barbie's gonna get you!" the older boy, Andrew, shouted, both boys collapsing gleefully on the floor as Rain leaped over that crazy dump truck driver, Barbie.

"What are you kids up to?" panted Sherry from the dining room where she was frantically dancing around the table, doing her aerobic exercises to Elton John songs that she played on the stereo with the arm up so that the side she liked better would repeat. The boys explained the magic of Azure-Rain as the creator of the wildly hilarious scenario. "Saturday, Saturday, Saturday night's all right!" Elton screamed over their laughter.

Sherry turned the volume down. "Those funny girls! Hey, let's make ants-on-a-log!"

"Mmmmmmmmmm," Sherry inhaled the smell of the peanut butter as we spread it on celery sticks, allowing herself one of the raisins we were lining up, six on each celery stick.

When Don got home from work he kissed Sherry, noogied her head, and squeezed her waist with both hands. "Dropping some of that weight," he commented approvingly. Hatchet-faced and stressed, she grinned and snarled like a hungry wolf and then started to cry.

I have to say that Sherry tried, but on top of everything else she had going on and no matter that we helped with cooking and watching the boys, we were just too much for her. I knew about some of the other things she had going on too, from listening to her talk with her sister over the phone: Don wasn't making any money; they needed a new furnace; she couldn't go to work because the babysitter would cost almost as much as she would make; even if they had an extra dollar, Don spent it going out with his friends; the kids were so wild, and getting cable for the TV would help but they couldn't afford it; the money from the County for fostering the girls helped but she never, ever got out, and it was so much work; the older one had so much trouble in school and the younger one was either pestering her or so quiet it spooked her.

"Azure-Rain," she said to me suddenly, "go find something to do. It's not nice to listen in when somebody's on the phone."

"Yes, the older one still wets the bed," I heard her say as I left the room. "Don thinks I should ask the County for a new washing machine because he says all that extra laundry is probably why ours is falling apart . . . he says if we can't get some help for all this work, they should just go back to the reservation . . ."

It was sometime during the summer after she went off cigarettes that we could see Sherry was losing heart. Things just added up one by one. When the boys started talking, Rainy began calling Sherry "Mama" just like they did, which made Sherry tell Rain not to call her Mama, just Sherry. Then Rainy asked if she knew where our real mother was.

"I'm not really sure," Sherry answered.

"Does that mean you know someplace she *might* be?" I asked. "Is she on the reservation?"

"Can we go see her?" asked Rain.

"Just never mind. It's snack time; I'm busy."

Sherry made peanut butter and jelly sandwiches and told us we could eat them in front of the TV for a change instead of the kitchen table. I let Rain and the boys sit close to the screen, and when I heard Sherry dialing the phone, I edged back around the doorway in order to hear what she was saying to her sister. She just couldn't keep up with everything, she said, never got used to having two other kids besides her own. It was more than double the work, and she had to fill out meal reports and clothes vouchers, and the last time the social worker stopped by the house was a terrible mess and she was sure the worker had heard her yelling at us to pick the place up before Don got home. And now the girls were asking about their mother. The County said she had given up her rights, but what if she found out where they were and just showed up at the house?

Sherry's sister had told her about a trick for quitting smoking: place a little pinch of tobacco in between her toes every morning. The nicotine would in theory get into her bloodstream and keep her from climbing the walls and going crazy. Don told Sherry that was just the kind of thing a lunatic like her sister would say — but what the hell, it might be worth a try. It surprised us all that it seemed to work, and although Sherry complained about putting on weight and that she was getting to be the size of a truck, Don told her he thought she looked better from the front, now that she was growing a bust.

· · ·

Near the end of the August when I was eight and Rainy nine, Sherry brightened up somewhat at the thought of school starting. She ordered school clothes, even our shoes, from the Penney's catalog, and then a week before the first day of school she gave all four of us haircuts that she found directions for in a magazine to neaten us up—the boys' shingled up the back and Rain's and mine parted in the middle and blunt-cut to bobs at midneck, all with thick heavy bangs down to the eyebrows. The boys' bangs reminded me of broom bristles; Rain's bangs covered her eyebrows and brought out the green of her eyes. My hair, as Sherry cut it, sprang into its natural wave, curving under at the ends. I loved it.

When Don got home that day, he asked her if she paid for that or did it herself—they looked like the Beatles.

"Hey, which one of you is Ringo?" he laughed.

Sherry dropped the basket of laundry she had just finished folding onto the floor, opened the storm door, and kicked the basket like a soccer ball out the door onto the porch and down the stairs.

Don told Azure-Rain to go bring that stuff inside. The boys thought it was a game.

"Azure-Rain, look! Look at my new hat!" Andrew twirled on the sidewalk with a pair of Don's undershorts on his head, waving a tube sock from each hand.

"Dad's underwear—ish!" Erik giggled, then tossed several balls of rolled-up socks at me; I caught them and placed them in the laundry basket. "Two! Six! Nineteen!" he shouted. "Bases loaded! . . . and sheeeeeee's out! Azure-Rain is out!"

Azure-Rain caught more socks and contained them in the basket; Azure-Rain gathered the clothes and folded them, except for Don's underwear—which I sternly told Andrew and Erik we would not touch because that was a job for boys.

"Butt-wear!" They picked up each piece between thumb and forefinger and dropped them into the basket.

"It's a boy job to carry the basket in the house, too." I sounded more authoritative than Sherry ever did, and Erik and Andrew cheerfully obeyed, one lifting a handle on each side. Then we went inside to eat one of our favorite suppers—Dinty Moore canned stew over mashed potatoes, with canned corn. Sherry showed Don the back-to-school-haircut article, and he said that he was just joking and that we looked good, as good as the barbershop. I patted my bob and pushed the ends up, feeling the satisfying weight of the curve and catching Sherry's eye.

"You look like the kids in the magazine," she said.

"Like school kids, for sure," said Don.

"I think Azure-Rain is beautiful." The expression of Erik's face was dopily smitten; I guess he must have just been wishing for someone to boss him around.

I think Rainy really believed we were each a half of one sister, Azure-Rain, and up until third or fourth grade it sometimes seemed that way to me as well: what one of us could do the other couldn't, and what one couldn't the other could. Rainy hated to read, yet she understood phonics and could sound out words; I loved to read yet stood dumbly when the teacher asked me to identify and sound out vowels and consonants. Rainy could not comprehend the meanings of sentences, what those strings of words were supposed to mean. I had learned to read by recognizing how words looked before I started kindergarten, yet once in first grade could not recognize those same words broken down into sounds and letters by phonetics. I struggled to learn letter by letter, sound by sound, chasing symbols that to my eyes ran in patterns up and down the page until I broke the code; Rainy never did and gave up. Yet she, the sister who could barely read, broke the numeral code right away, easily mastering addition, subtraction, multiplication, and division until she was tricked, as she saw it, by Miss Fisketti.

Miss Fisketti lied about the remainder.

Rainy had discovered, after explaining to me about the remainder for two entire afternoon walks home after school ("And what's left over after division is called the remainder! You write it down, right there at the top, a little *r* and what's left over and that's called the remainder, it's what remains after the problem, is what Miss Fisketti said!"), that the remainder was not really the remainder at all and thus not the end of the problem: it would have to be divided up into fractions or decimal points. After all that work and sequenced following of directions, which never came easily to her, Rainy had been betrayed. And by Miss Fisketti of all people, Miss Fisketti who smelled so nice and wore such pretty clothes.

As I heard it being discussed by the principal and Sherry an hour later, my older younger sister had raised her hand for permission to go to the washroom, communicating to Miss Fisketti the secret sign she had taught the students to indicate the length of time that their bathroom visits would require: across her chest Rain had held up two fingers in a sideways V (indicating a request for a longer stay than the one finger sign). Stuffed down the front of Rainy's jeans and covered by her sweater were her math worksheets from the beginning of the school year, which the students kept stacked inside their desks for what Miss Fisketti called "the building blocks of arithmetic." Alone in the girls' washroom, Rainy had removed one worksheet and then rolled the rest into a thick tube that she stuffed as far as she could into the toilet without getting her hands wet and flushed.

The monitor from the principal's office had knocked on the door to my classroom and handed a note to my teacher, Mr. Anderson, who unlike Miss Fisketti smelled like stale polyester pants and days-old socks. The room was quiet because we were copying a paragraph out in cursive, and although the room remained quiet as the monitor walked purposefully and importantly to the teacher's desk, all of our heads and eyes, as if attached to a single cord pulled by the monitor, turned to see the distraction. The teacher looked up and glanced my way a few times as he read the note; with each glance my stomach took small cold leaps in anticipation of all that might be wrong.

Mr. Anderson, who was actually pretty nice, walked to my desk to tell me in a quiet voice that was intended to protect my privacy, although every ear in the room, strung to that single cord now pulled by my dancing stomach, was turned to listen. "Azure, you are needed in the office."

Whispers rippled across the room. The snotty girl next to me raised her eyebrows. From the back a boy's voice, "What did she do?" and a reply, "Whoa—busted."

"Back to your work, people. Take your coat and your backpack along, Azure. Don't forget your homework."

The door to the inner office was closed, but through its mesh-enforced window I could see the thin back of our foster mother, who was perched at the edge of her chair with Erik on one knee and Andrew on the other. Sherry was gesturing nervously as she talked with the principal, whose hands were folded under his chin. Outside the door, five brightly colored plastic chairs were arranged in what was meant to be a friendly half-circle; Rain sat in the cheerily tangerine-orange chair at the end farthest from the door, her head down, talking to her hands that twisted and drummed on her knees. "Liar," she was saying. "Liar, liar, liar." She punched her backpack, which had been placed on the sunshine-yellow chair next to her.

I sat in the center chair, a happy sky blue that was my favorite color. Rain looked up. "She's a liar. Miss Fisketti lied. She's a liar," she said.

"What did she lie about?"

"The remainder. There isn't any such thing. First she said there was, and then she said there wasn't. She said we had to divide it up because it wasn't real. Miss Fisketti lied." Rainy opened her backpack and took out a worksheet, which she handed to me. "See? I saved this one to show you. From Tuesday. I got them all right. But they're really all wrong. Because she lied."

Each long division problem on the sheet had been painstakingly worked out in Rainy's careful numerals. Every number was carefully contained in its invisible—to Rainy's mind, visible—box, and penciled so forcefully that each was a shiny, number-shaped dent in the paper. Next to each answer was a letter *r*, again a shiny dent, and the number left over from the long division problem. Across the top of the paper Miss Fisketti had written "All correct! Good job!" and had drawn a smiley face.

"See? She lied."

At supper that evening, as Sherry slapped a second helping of hotdish—another of our favorites: canned tuna, egg noodles, mushroom soup, and canned corn—onto his plate, Don asked her why the hell she sat and took that kind of crap from the school, and why she didn't just tell them to take a hike? Who did they think they were, jerking her around like that, making her walk all that way to listen to that shit.

"And I cannot believe that you apologized to that bucket-assed old maid of a principal. Why in the hell should you apologize to him? You didn't do anything!"

"Rain did it!" Erik chimed in helpfully. His dad told everybody to shut up and eat, which was just as well because Rainy's explanation wouldn't have helped. We both kept our eyes on our plates and on getting through our delicious although this time ever so slightly sticky mounds of tuna, egg noodles, and corn held together with cream of mushroom soup.

Sherry rapped the excess hotdish off the spoon against the side of the Pyrex mixing bowl and then wiped some from Andrew's mouth with her shirt tail. "Forgot to rinse the noodles," she mumbled to herself. Then she sat and stared at her husband.

"I don't know," she said.

"You don't know what?"

"I don't know why I apologized to the principal. I don't know anything. You're right." Sherry scraped the bottom of the bowl with her butter knife and ate the crunchy remainder of the tuna hotdish like potato chips.

"About what?"

"Everything."

"So go ahead and clam up, that always helps. Jeeeeezus." Don buttered a slice of bread, bit off half of it, and chewed.

What really turned the corner for Sherry happened the following summer at the grocery store. Summers were hard on Sherry because we were all on vacation from school, and because Rain and I belonged to the County, she could never leave us by ourselves but had to take us everywhere she went. During the school year a trip to the grocery, or anywhere else, wasn't such a big deal, especially after the boys were old enough for school; she went by herself and had a nice time in her own company. Summers, however, she had to bring all four of us with her wherever she went, even though Rain and I would have been happy to stay at home and babysit Erik and Andrew.

The summertime grocery store trips had become increasingly hectic since the boys had grown big enough to walk by themselves because they always wanted to run around, so Sherry had developed a system that she used on the days she'd had enough and she really meant it this time, as she would say. The rule was that Erik had to hold Rain's hand and Andrew mine from the car into the store, while she found a cart. Only when she lifted each little boy into one cart were they allowed to let go of our hands.

"Your butts have to be touching the bottom of the grocery cart at all times," she reminded them as firmly as she could. Erik lifted his legs and waved his feet over the side.

"And hands and feet inside at all times." Andrew pulled Erik's Minnesota Twins hat down to his chin.

"And hands to yourself. Or your dad will hear about it." I knew that would buy her about two minutes of good behavior.

Sherry grabbed the handle of a second cart from the dozen stuck together near the door. That one would be Rainy's to push; my job was to take the things that Sherry wanted and put them into Rainy's cart. We always tried to make it as easy as we could for Sherry, but what happened next that particular day threw her off and, eventually, led to our lives changing yet again.

The cart was stuck. Right behind us, two Native women, both older and crabbier-looking than Sherry, waited their turn as she fumbled clumsily and jerked at the handle with her skinny, fine-boned hands. One finally stepped right in front of Sherry and gave the cart a good yank, freeing it and pushing it towards us.

"Here," she said.

"Oh, that's yours," Sherry answered, flustered.

"You can take it; you've got kids, go ahead."

"Thanks. Rain, here's your cart."

"Hey, you." This from the second woman. "Where did you get these kids? Are they yours?" Both women stared at Sherry, with her thick blonde hair like straw and her little boys with their heavy straw-blonde Beatles bangs hanging straight down to their eyebrows, then at Rainy and me.

Sherry smiled nervously. I tried to help. "We're foster girls."

"Where are they from? Are they from Mozhay? Did you take them from there?"

"I don't really know—we have to get going."

"What makes you think you're the only one who can take care of them? How much are you getting paid?" The second woman again. "Did you ever think they might have their own family?"

"Liz, let's go inside," her friend said. "Come on, Liz."

"Stealing Indian kids, who the hell do you people think you are, that you think you can just do that?"

"Liz, leave her alone. It's not her fault."

A dirty look from Liz, who muttered *baby stealers* and *boarding school haircuts* as the two walked into the grocery store.

Rainy's eyes were round as wheels. "Do we know those ladies?"

"Are we Indians?" Andrew seemed very excited about the possibility.

We left the grocery store and returned home without buying groceries. Sherry lined us all up on the couch and turned on Oprah. Then she went into the kitchen, where she began fixing another of our favorite suppers: canned chili over rice, with canned peas on the side and fruit cocktail with graham crackers for dessert.

"Do you think Sherry stole us?" Rain whispered to me.

When Don got home Sherry told him she needed to talk to him, privately. I listened outside their bedroom door to Sherry crying and Don shouting something about those slobs, those dirty old Indians, dirty old bags, couldn't take care of their own kids, and then Sherry crying harder and finally Don coming out and shutting the door very softly.

Don told us that Sherry needed to lie down for a little while upstairs, that maybe she would come down for supper.

"What kind of pizza do you like, Azure-Rain?" he asked me.

"I'm Azure, she's Rain. Pepperoni."

"Azure, right. What kind do you want, Rain? How about sausage?"

He called Domino's and ordered a bottle of Sprite and two pizzas, one pepperoni and one sausage. While we waited for the pizza guy, he asked us how we liked school.

"Not very much," I answered.

"Miss Fisketti is a liar," said my little big sister. "She lied about the remainder."

"What?" asked Don.

"When Sherry had to go to the principal's office that time. It was because Miss Fisketti lied to us." And then she told Don the whole story. He was, it seemed, a good listener when the person talking wasn't Sherry.

It took Don to explain things. The remainder, he said, was like leftover pizza: you could put what you didn't eat in the fridge, and that was the remainder. You could hang on to the remainder for a while, and even wrap it in plastic and stick it in the freezer for a while longer—but it would eventually get eaten by somebody. If it was one person, then it would be one whole serving of the remainder; if it was two people sharing the leftovers then it would be two servings out of the remainder, or half; if it was three people then it would be three out of the remainder, which would be one-third each.

To be fair to Miss Fisketti, he told us, it wasn't her fault that she didn't think about how the remainder worked in real life. She was probably book smart but not real-life smart. But that didn't mean a person could go around plugging up the toilet at school, he said to Rain.

It was the first time Don had ever actually talked to us, and he didn't seem so bad. He was always so crabby when he talked to Sherry, and I never could quite figure out why.

With some backup from Don, Sherry managed to have Rain referred for a special education assessment. I heard Sherry tell her sister over the phone that the assessment report didn't turn up any particular disability that could be diagnosed, and that Rain didn't meet any "categorical criteria, they said, whatever that means." Thinking the situation might improve if we were together, the teachers moved me to the same classroom as my sister. Rain learned to read and write, in her way, as well as to keep quiet about the inconsistencies of math and science.

When the boys were old enough to start school and wouldn't need to spend so much time—and Sherry and Don's money—at a babysitter's, Sherry decided that she wouldn't be able to keep us and told me that she liked having us around but had decided to go back to work. We both knew that this was not untrue but also not the entire story. I didn't hold it against her. Not long after that, she told us we would be going to live at a new foster house. She washed and sorted all our clothes, which she stuffed into one large black plastic trash bag, as instructed by the County; she sorted our school papers and our toys into another trash bag early one morning. As we ate breakfast before the social worker was to pick us up, Erik burst into a sudden storm of weeping that slopped, along with his teary, dripping nose, into his bowl of Quisp.

"I don't want you to go," he cried.

I told him how much fun it would be for him to have his very own room. Sherry added that Don was going to paint it blue, like outer space, that she would draw little stars in with a pencil that would leave sparkles. He cried harder.

Andrew, his face all scrunched up like his dad's did most of the time when he looked at Sherry, said that he didn't want his own room.

"It will be so fun, you can spread out and do whatever you want," Sherry said. "And Azure-Rain will, too, at their new place. Everybody will have fun!"

Rain opened one of the black trash bags and dug out two naked Barbie dolls. "Here, you can play war with the Barbies, and they can drive the dump truck and fight crime," she said.

When the County worker came to pick us up we were all of us— Sherry, Erik, Andrew, me, and Rain—waiting on the front stairs, Rain and I each with a plastic garbage bag at our feet, and Erik and Andrew each with a naked Barbie clutched in a sweaty fist.

"Good-bye, Andrew! Good-bye, Erik!" we called from the open

car window as we drove away. Andrew and Erik held and waved their Barbies, holding them high in the air.

"Good-bye, Sherry!" We still didn't call her Mama.

Our next foster mother was Mrs. Kukonen, and we stayed at her house in the townships outside of Mesabi for four years until, as she told us, the Indians decided they wanted us back and they could just have us—that she'd be a lot better off renting out the upstairs than waiting on a couple of lazy, sloppy, ungrateful snots twenty-four hours a day.

Mrs. Kukonen, who we never thought of calling Mama, never got us mixed up like Sherry and the boys did, and called us Rainfall and Azure when we were outside the house. Inside, though, she had her own names for us, and it wasn't long before it didn't seem unnatural at all to be addressed as Miss Stuck-up and Miss Pee Pot, or to being occasionally slapped and pushed, in a rhythm tandem to the pronunciation of those names. When we would leave Mrs. Kukonen's four years later and go to Dolly's, we had to get used to being called Rainy and Azure at home all over again.

Rainy had just turned fourteen and I was almost thirteen when the County told Mrs. Kukonen that we were moving to another foster home because of the Indian Child Welfare Act. It was the law, she told us. Somebody we were related to had requested us.

Our mother, I breathed to myself.

"God knows who these people are, but they're going to be your fosters now." Mrs. Kukonen snorted. "Good luck with that, is all I have to say."

Not our mother. With that second breath my chest sank.

"I just told that snot at the County and I had been going to tell them I couldn't keep them anymore, anyway," Mrs. Kukonen said, speaking to herself or some invisible person in that habit she had, "but she beat me to it. What if one of them ended up pregnant, especially that younger one, and why couldn't they figure out what was the matter with the older one? If she isn't retarded, it sure is something else. And another thing: how in the world some Indian is going to be able to do a better job with those girls and all the troubles they have is beyond me. All I can do is wish them luck, I said to the County," she told herself and the invisible person as we ate our Hamburger Helper. "They're in for some surprise when they get a load of you-know-who."

Rainy took a gulp of water to wash down a congealing spoonful of Hamburger Helper. "Who?" she asked.

Mrs. Kukonen sniffed and swallowed (she was always stuffed up because of her allergies). "See what I mean?" she asked the invisible person. "Fodder for Hell," she mumbled down to her plate.

We hadn't especially liked Mrs. Kukonen since the day we arrived at her house, even before she renamed us. She made Rainy sleep on an Army cot with an old plastic shower curtain under the sheet because Rainy still wet the bed, and she didn't care that we were afraid of her runny-eyed, ancient Siamese cat Soo-Soo, who slept with Mrs. Kukonen, draining his yellow eye pus all night long on the pillow right next to her head and got up early in the morning to drag himself upstairs to leave hard little turds that she called "Tootsie Rolls" on our blankets. Soo-Soo's ears gave off a mildew smell, and he gorged his Little Friskies and vomited on the kitchen rug, the one shaped like an orange slice, and she still treated him nicer than she treated Rainy. Mrs. Kukonen would stretch a pound of ground beef over three boxes of Hamburger Helper; it looked like Soo-Soo's regurgitated Little Friskies, and we ate it for supper almost every night. She never bought brownie mix or canned chili or stew or potatoes; she said that they were garbage and a waste of money. She never let me and Rain cook, because we would just dirty up the kitchen. She did, however, let us wash the dishes—but not waste the dish detergent, which she measured carefully, herself, three drops and not one more, into the dishpan—and dry them with greasy-feeling dish towels.

Mrs. Kukonen kept the furnace vent to the upstairs closed, and on winter mornings Rainy shivered in her sleep, chilled in cold urine puddled on the sheet. Worst of all (or so I thought, until when Mrs. Kukonen hurt Rainy's face), the whole house, all of the furniture and even the towels and pillows, smelled like Soo-Soo's cat box and hardboiled eggs.

On Sundays, unless the weather was bad, we walked down the road to church—God's Eternal Sinners Saved—dressed in white blouses and denim jumpers given to us by one of the church ladies whose daughter had grown to adulthood. The jumpers were tent-like and pleated across the chest in front and back, with six-inch hems that were let down as we grew. We sat near the front, one on either side of Mrs. Kukonen, through two lengthy services every Sunday that we looked forward to because while the pastor was speaking you never knew who might stand up next to talk about their own sins. The Eternal Sinners did worse things than wet the bed: their stories were more lurid than the programs on TV that were Mrs. Kukonen's sinful pleasure and a secret from the rest of the Sinners. Although we couldn't actually see it happen with our own eyes, no matter what they had done, God forgave them every single time, right there in church, once he heard the details (and how we enjoyed the details they shared, egged on by their fellow Sinners Saved, many of whom also backslid every so often). "Praise the Lord!" the pastor would proclaim, wrinkling his nose that was raised toward heaven and looked oddly like Don's when he looked at Sherry. "Hallelujah!" Rainy and I would shout, along with the other Sinners.

The two Sunday services and the Wednesday evening Godly Girls Guild were the extent of our social life. We didn't socialize outside of school; Mrs. Kukonen's house was out in the country, and she didn't want to spend time and gas money driving us around. It was bad enough on Wednesdays, she thought, making the drive when the weather was bad and waiting while we dillydallied around, but at least we were with decent girls, unlike the Lord our Savior only knew what kind of girls we spent our days with at school. So on Wednesdays we hustled, gobbling our supper and cleaning things up as fast as we could before donning our musty-smelling seldom-washed denim jumpers.

It was always a relief to get back to Mrs. Kukonen's after church or GGG and change out of those droopy denim coverall jumpers and back into our everyday clothes. Every year for school Mrs. Kukonen used our County vouchers to buy us each two pairs of wide-legged polyester pants with elastic waists, two white blouses, and a sweater vest to cover our chests for the sake of modesty. For after school and Saturdays we wore last year's outfits, which were almost the same as the current year's except that they were smaller and a little beat-up looking. For all the limits of our wardrobes, we felt much more stylish while at the same time more modest than the other girls at the Sinners, who wore dresses all the time, even for play. It was the Lord's rule, they told us.

I thought that rule was really strange since we climbed trees and chased each other around the church grounds during the break between Sunday services, and some of the girls liked to hang from the biggest tree branch by their knees, with their oversized white panties showing to the entire world. I suppose the Sinners thought that was all right because the boys and girls were always separated during play time—but I know that the boys, especially the older ones, took a good look whenever the adults weren't watching.

The County social worker probably deserved the credit for our secular outfits, which some of the other Godly Girls admired for their style and freedom of movement. "You are so lucky you get to wear pants to school," sighed Charity, who wore the same heavily ruffled homemade prairie-style dresses to school that she did to the services at Sinners, and who before she hung upside down from the tree branch modestly bunched the back hem of her full skirt into a fistful of cloth that she pulled up between her knees and tucked into her sash in front. "I'm not allowed to wear pants. It's forbidden by the Lord."

"You don't wear pants?" gasped Rainy in shock.

"She means slacks, not underpants . . . right, Charity?"

Following Rain's thoughts and the sinful pictures in our heads, Charity's mouth opened and closed at the horror of our questions. At the next Godly Girls Guild she got in the spirit during prayer: jumping into the center of the circle of GGGs with linked arms she began to twirl, hopping up and down, pointing to the ceiling, and squeaking. She told us later that she had been moved to reach her hand to the Lord our Savior on our behalf.

"Thank you, Charity," I said, hoping she wasn't expecting us to return the favor.

"It's my duty, my mother says. She prays for you, too. She says the Lord only knows what kind of Satan's work the Indians did to you in the first place, but you can still be saved and not have to burn in Hell for eternity."

"We'll pray for you, too, won't we, Rain?"

Sweet Charity hugged me. "I just know the Lord is going to touch you!"

Rain had a smile that was a little off-center, her mouth a little weaker on one side. In repose she looked sad, as if her eyes would fill with tears in a moment and she would cry; when she was actually on the verge of tears, though, she looked as though she might start laughing.

It was Mrs. Kukonen who had put the crimp at the side of

Rainy's mouth. One night when we were watching the news on TV, a car commercial came on. "Dare to compare! Toyota-thon!" sang the jubilant dancers in the studio's pretend car dealership. "Dare, dare to compare! Dare!"

"Dare to compare!" exclaimed the announcer.

Rainy raised her arms, palms out, just like the minister who looked even more like Don when he was in the Word. "Praise the Lord our Savior!" she boomed in his voice.

Mrs. Kukonen backhanded Rainy so hard that her mouth split between her upper and lower lips on the right side, and her nose bled. "Never, ever take the Lord's name in vain!" she snapped. That side of Rainy's face was numb for months, and the tooth just in back of her right eye tooth eventually grayed and fell out. When everything had healed over, she had developed a slight lisp when she spoke, a loose-sounding sideways sputter on the right side, and the permanent crimp at the side of her mouth gave Rainy a smile that was slightly crooked and knowing, like she was in on a secret.

But Rain didn't smile that much after that, and neither did I. Or talk. We didn't have much to say, ever, which was fine with Mrs. Kukonen.

I really could hardly believe it when she told us that the Indians were taking us away on account of the Indian Child Welfare Act (when she pronounced the words, Mrs. Kukonen said "welfare" a little more loudly than the others). It was almost as though one of the miracles that happened at the Sinners was bursting forth from God's merciful hand right there in Mrs. Kukonen's smelly house. I was almost tempted to raise my hands, palms out to the holiness of the spirit, and shout, "Thank you, Jesus!"

But I didn't, and neither did my sister. During our years at Mrs. Kukonen's Rainy had become cured of her willful and defiant ways to a point that satisfied our foster mother, and we had become used to the idea that we might have to live with her until we turned eighteen, which seemed so far off that it might have been forever. I could hardly believe our good luck that we were being taken away, though I kept that to myself around Mrs. Kukonen, and I thought there might really be a God, after all, and that he had showered his unmerited favor upon two undeserving sister sinners. Just because he felt guilty about letting the County place us with Mrs. Kukonen in the first place.

And so I rejoiced, my leaps of euphoria invisible, even to Rain, who I could hear in the middle of the night thanking Jesus herself, her lateral lisp soft and fervent as she lay on her cold rubber-sheeted cot in the closet.

Just the same, when it was time to go, we were afraid to leave. Our life at Mrs. Kukonen's house, miserable though it had been, was what we had become used to—we had come to think of her smelly house as home. Except for Rainy wetting the bed, we hadn't been much trouble at all, I thought. There were lots of foster kids worse than us, I thought. Then the back of my neck felt cold and shivery as I thought, *And lots of foster homes besides Mrs. Kukonen's.* Where might the County send us next?

On the day we left, we waited on the soft, mildew-smelling front stairs quiet as dread—me watching ants crawl over and chew on a dead beetle, and Rainy pulling scabs off the mosquito bites on her ankles.

The social worker pulled up in a little red car, a Chevy that looked new. She was young and pretty; her long hair bounced and furled like yellow curling ribbons as she got out of the car. "Hi, girls," she called. "Are you Rainfall and Azure? I'm here to pick you up!"

Mrs. Kukonen stuck her head out the screen door. "You might as well come in; there's a lot to haul away."

"I'm Samantha Grimsby," the social worker said, offering her hand. Mrs. Kukonen took it limply for a second or so and dropped it.

"I can't lift a thing with my bad back." Mrs. Kukonen eyed the social worker's fingernails, which were long and painted a bright pink, clearly a temptation to the devil.

Rainy and I each carried our things in a heavy-duty black trash bag, and Mrs. Kukonen handed a paper grocery bag to the social worker. "Their school papers are in there," she said.

"Call me Sammy, girls." The social worker's eyebrows raised just a little and her nose wrinkled just a little more at the eggy cat-box smell in Mrs. Kukonen's house, but she kept right on smiling. "Let's put everything in the hatchback." We piled our trash bags on top of the spare tire, and Sammy wedged the grocery bag next to a briefcase. "Pew," she said under her breath but turned to smile at us. "Who wants to ride in the front seat?"

Rainy did. I sat in back with my feet square on the floor and looked straight ahead, but Rainy squirmed and knelt to see out the rear window as we drove away, waving to Mrs. Kukonen, who was probably turned away and walking back to the house to watch *As the World Turns* with Soo-Soo. The car turned a corner; my stomach dipped, flipped, and I wished I was sitting on the couch next to Soo-Soo, breathing through my mouth to minimize the smell that was at least familiar.

With Mrs. Kukonen's house out of sight, Rainy smiled her crooked smile as she settled into the front seat, playing with the shoulder harness. "It smells good in here, doesn't it, Azh?"

I inhaled the sharp freshness of new car, ashamed of our own scent of Kukonen household.

The social worker turned on the radio to a station we liked but weren't allowed to listen to at Mrs. Kukonen's. Humming along to the pop songs, she asked us questions every few minutes about school. What subjects did we like the best, she asked, and what was our favorite lunch? I didn't say much, but Rainy, basking in the attention, told Samantha all about my love of macaroni and cheese and hers of fish sticks, that I wished for a pair of jeans with embroidery on the back pockets, and that she, Rainy, hoped our new foster mother was nice.

"She is," Samantha said with the enthusiasm of someone who wasn't going to have to go to a new foster home herself. "And she is really excited that you will be coming back to live in Duluth."

"What's it like there?" I asked.

"We-e-e-e-ell . . . Her name is Dolly, and she lives with her son, Vernon—she calls him Junior—and he is your cousin, second- or third-cousin, or something like that."

"How old is he? Is he a kid?"

"No-o-o-o-o . . . he's an adult, and he works at a job and takes care of his mother. And they will both take care of you."

"Is she old, like Mrs. Kukonen?"

"She is an older lady; I suppose she would be about a grand-mother age. She has a little dog. Do you like little dogs?"

"I do," said Rainy. "I love little dogs, but I'm scared if they're mean."

"Have you been to their house?" I asked. So she was an old lady, like Mrs. Kukonen—whose eggy Soo-Soo house smell was stinking up Samantha's pretty car.

"Yes, I have. The house has a porch, and a garage, and a patio in the backyard with a picnic table. And they have fixed up a room for you girls to share; when I was there Vernon was painting the walls, and they bought all new sheets and a really pretty comforter, wait till you see it . . ."

What would happen when Rain wet the bed? I turned my face to the side window, filled with dread, picturing the disgust and wrath of our new foster mother when she discovered the new bedding wet with urine.

Samantha reached back past the console to pat my knee and turned up the radio. "Oh, do you girls like this song?" she asked.

"We don't listen to this station at home."

"The words are easy; want to sing it with me? Come on, it's fun!"

By the time we arrived at our foster placement, Rainy, Sammy, and Cyndi Lauper were nearing the end of "Girls Just Wanna Have Fun."

They just a-wanna, they just a-wanna-a-a. They just a-wanna, they just a-wanna-a-a.

Duluth

DOLLY

If we had known when it was that Loretta vanished, we might have been able to find her. I know that Buster would have done what he could, for sure; him and Patsy felt just terrible. Junior, once he found out, would have moved heaven and earth, but by then it was too late. It seemed Loretta had just vanished into thin air.

The sorry fact is that when Albert brought that little girl to Miskwaa, the circumstances were so sad, with her mother, Frances, being a bad alcoholic like that and Albert a drinker himself and not much better, both of them fighting whenever they saw each other about everything and, when they thought about it, their daughter, too.

Loretta would have been better off with Buster and Patsy, for sure, and even though it was hard for Patsy, she could have done it—raised Albert and Frances's girl along with her own children. Loretta's life would have been so different from how it turned out. She would have gone to school with Artense, watched over by Patsy like a miser with a bag of gold, might have graduated and gone to college or to work. It might have even made Artense's life easier, with somebody her own age to do things with, and Loretta could have been a big help to Patsy, too.

But that is not the way it happened. Instead, Albert and Loretta got as far as Mozhay Point, where he left his little girl with Grace Dionne, who kept an eye on her for a while. Then the County showed up one day after Grace had called them to ask what she should do with this little girl, and the County took Loretta to Miskwaa because it turned out that Frances wanted Loretta back. In my opinion what Frances really wanted was the monthly aid check from the County that came along with Loretta—but as she put it, nobody could take care of her little girl the way she, Frances, could; nobody could love her the way she, Frances, could. And besides that, Patsy was so snobbish with her nose in the air and her big plans for her and Buster's kids, telling everybody that Artense was going to be a doctor and then that she was going to be a teacher. The Gallettes at Miskwaa River tended to agree with Frances on that.

The fact is that Loretta only stayed with Frances or Albert from time to time, and in between she was in foster placement here and there and all over the place. At some point she lost that sparkle she had and became so quiet that she all but stopped speaking, and then in her early teens she began to get into angry confrontations and physical fights. That was the last time I saw her, when she was about thirteen and a real pack of trouble. In the foster system she moved from placement to placement, palmed off on whoever would take her in, until they got tired of her and then palmed her off on somebody else. When she turned eighteen, Loretta was completely on her own, scrounging money, food, and places to live God knows where.

Just days after Louis's funeral, Junior had left Duluth for his new assignment in Germany. From there—and I never knew he was doing this until he had everything nailed down, which still gripes me when I think about it—he wrote a letter to Artense asking her about Loretta. It was Artense who then kept in touch with Junior, writing when she heard that Loretta had had a baby, a boy, while living in Duluth and that the baby had been adopted out, and that two years later Loretta had another baby, this one a girl and then not much more than a year later a third baby, this one born up at Mesabi.

Sept. 14, 1984

Dear Junior,

Well, it's been a while since I've written—got your postcard and was glad to hear from you—I showed the picture of the castle to Jenny and Michelle, and then showed them on the map where Germany is. They are getting big, and we are fine here—it was quite a change, moving to the Iron Range, but we are getting used to it and we are going to try to buy a house. Stan likes his job and I am working part-time a few nights a week at the movies, doing concessions.

The reason it took me so long to write is I was trying to find an answer to your question about Loretta—I asked Aunt Shirley, since she does driving for Indian Health Service in Duluth and so she gets around a lot and knows a lot of people. Here is what she knows, and maybe you already know some of it: First, nobody has seen Loretta in a long time. We would run into her every once in a while when she was mostly living in Duluth, but she moved around, you know how it is, so she was at Mozhay sometimes and also in Minneapolis, and she went to treatment at least once but didn't stay and went back to drinking. As far as Shirley knows she hadn't been to Miskwaa River for a long time, Shirley doesn't know why but thinks it has something to do with the father of her second baby. And Loretta's mother, Frances— you know Loretta didn't spend much time with her when we were kids—anyway, after Frances moved to Minneapolis and Albert died, Loretta didn't go back to Miskwaa again, as far as anybody knows. I hate telling you about this but you

asked and so I will—Shirley says things were really hard for
Loretta, and the County finally was going to take away her
two little girls—she signed them away, since she was going to
lose them, and nobody has seen her since around that time.
Shirley is asking around and I will write to you when she
finds out anything. Sorry this is so short but it took me such a
long time to write that I think I should get this in the mail.

Cousin Artense

Junior didn't save a lot of things, probably because his Army career moved him around to a new assignment every couple of years.
He carried very little from base to base but occasionally shipped a
box home for me to keep for him. Although I unpacked the boxes,
I never read his letters or papers, thinking if he wanted me to he
would say so. Instead, as soon as each box arrived, I brought it into
the storage room opening off the kitchen where I kept my sewing.
Touching each thing, every single postcard, letter, souvenir, photo
of Vernon at work or with his friends, as though it was a bit of my
son himself, I stacked them, the letters remaining unread on the
shelves of the room that Junior could have as his own special, private place for mementos when he'd retired—his place for reading
or listening to the radio. Junior's den, I called it to myself.

If I had read some of the letters he saved, I would have known
that Junior had not forgotten about Loretta at all. It was just before he
retired from the Service that I finally found out what he and Artense
had been up to and that Shirley Pomeroy had also become involved,
in other words, stuck her nose where she just assumed it was her
business and helped Junior try to track down Loretta's children. For
an operator like Shirley it was a piece of cake, especially with help
from her niece Artense, who in spite of her touch-me-not nose-in-
the-air ways was just as big a busybody as her aunt. With the two of
them thick as thieves it was like a little Mafia operation—Shirley
operating from Duluth, where she drove everybody in town around

in the Indian Health Service van, gossiping all day long better than a radio program, and Artense from up north on the Range, where she was close to the reservation and her cousin Dale Ann Dionne.

April 30, 1985

Dear Junior,

I know you have heard from Shirley that she went to the police station and reported Loretta as missing, and that is as far as anything has gone—the police told her that they keep a regular eye out for missing persons. Shirley wonders if it's possible that Loretta might just show up one day. Her daughters— Dale Ann has asked Fred Simon, who is on the RBC (do you know Fred? He was sweet on Dale Ann when they were kids, I think, but he married a girl from the Cities—anyway, he is the Sweetgrass District representative) if they can use the Indian Child Welfare Act to make St. Louis County give the children back to her family—that means you, of course.

Went down to Duluth for the Ni-M-Win powwow at the Bayfront—Uncle Tommy was camped out close to the powwow circle, had his tent set up and his truck parked right behind it. Cousin Bobby was there from Grand Portage, and he was wearing a vest and leggings that his mom had beaded on when he was a little boy. Shirley asked me to dance with her— she dances traditional and it was such a nice time. Tommy kept a little campfire going and coffee on, so he had a lot of company stopping by, as you can probably imagine.

We are fine here, hope you are, too. I am cashiering at the drugstore now, 5:00–9:00, so I have supper ready early and eat before Stan gets home from work, then I take off and get there before 5:00 if I can so the day cashier can leave on time—it's only about three blocks from home, so I walk there. It's fun there—the owner, Mr. Shapiro, knows my Aunt Martha and he is nice.

I hope you are ready for a big party when you get home—
everybody is really excited to see you, and Auntie Babe and
my mom have been arguing over whose house it is going to
be at—so far it looks like Auntie Babe is winning but only
because Patsy decided to let her. They don't have a date yet but
we'll come down to Duluth whenever it is, me and Stan and
the girls—it is funny that you will be a little old retired man,
haha (yes, I know you are 39).

    Shirley says to tell you she is going to find those babies. I
will write just as soon as we find anything out, and once you
are in the States let us know how we can reach you by phone.

                         Little Cousin Artense

I would do anything for Junior, and I don't want anyone to think
I didn't want Loretta's girls. Junior sprang it on me, there's no other
way to put it, on the way home after I picked him up at the Grey-
hound station; my first thought was that it was the kind of thing
Maggie would have done, and that it was no surprise at all that
Junior had inherited her goodness and Vernon's sweetness. And I
could understand when he said he'd wanted to tell me in person; I
admit I was jealous, thinking about how Artense and Shirley were
in on this before me, but over the years I had learned that there
are some things that I call "Indian things" when it comes to that
whole family bunch—the Gallettes and the Robineaus and the La-
Forces just seem to have some kind of connection to every Indian
in the whole world, and I just have to let it be. I had been thinking,
before the drive back to the house from the bus depot, that with
Junior finally home for good he'd marry some nice young woman
from Duluth or Mozhay one of these days and they would give me
some grandchildren; they might even buy the house next door to
ours when the old widower who owned it decided to sell, or died.
Instead, what Junior had been working on was a different kind of
addition to the family—and after many phone calls and letters an

official home visit from Fred Simon, who represented Sweetgrass as the elected member of the Mozhay Point Reservation Business Committee, was arranged. This was followed by an appeal to the RBC, which voted to approve a letter from the tribal chairman to the County requesting that Loretta Gallette's children be returned to her family under the terms of the Indian Child Welfare Act. The County, not contesting the request, assessed and licensed Junior and me as home foster caregivers; and those two shy little teenagers, Azure Sky and Rainfall Dawn, poor lost Loretta's daughters, were reassigned by the Mozhay Point RBC and the County foster care system to Junior.

It was the law, after all. As Shirley told the RBC when she and Junior made their request at Mozhay: "It's just since 1978 that we've had the Indian Child Welfare Act, and it was a long hard road to getting there. The Indian people are in grief for the loss of so many of our children. Loretta Gallette was one of those children; she is still lost. Please help us get her children back to our family and tribe."

AZURE SKY

The gray-shingled house on Duluth's western hillside was single-story, not a two-story like Mrs. Kukonen's, and set on a crowded narrow lot. The front yard was shortened by an added deck that extended halfway to the sidewalk; most of the rest was taken up by a large white cement birdbath flanked by two swan planters. On the deck a woman sat in a webbed lawn chair, smoking. With one hand she held her cigarette; with the other she cradled a pink bundle. Did she have a baby? Her own or a foster? As we pulled up to the house that first day, our new foster mother stood and we saw that she looked a lot older than Sherry, maybe older than Mrs. Kukonen. She tossed the cigarette in the grass, fumbled on her chest for her glasses that hung on a jeweled cord, put them on and peered at us, then walked to the passenger side of the car cradling the pink bundle that whimpered and squeaked. Somewhat uncertainly she patted her fluffy yellow hair into place, then held her hand out to the social worker, who shook it with her own manicured hand and asked, "Mrs. Gallette? I'm Samantha Grimsby, from St. Louis County, and I have brought Azure Sky and Rainfall Dawn. Girls, this is Dolly Gallette."

"Same last name as ours," I whispered to Rainy.

"Azh, I don't think she's our real mother," Rainy whispered back.

The bundle yipped once, twice—it was a little dog, not a baby. Rainy tensed up, expecting the woman to put the dog down to snap and bite at her ankles, but the woman only whispered sharply *Shhh! No barking!* and touched the end of its quivering black nose with her index finger. The dog, the size of Soo-Soo, silenced and snuggled into the crook of the woman's arm like a baby. It even had a hairdo like a baby, with bangs under a little ponytail tied up into a pink-ribbon bow.

"Look what I've got here," the woman said in a high voice like Cyndi Lauper's. "Isn't she teensy? You little cookies ever seen a Yorkie? This one loves girls." She gently waved one of the dog's tiny paws. "Say hello, Jennifer. Hello to the girls." She held the dog in front of her own mouth and pretended the little thing was talking. "Hello-o-o-o-o-o, girls," she said in her pretend-Jennifer voice, slightly higher and squeakier than Cyndi Lauper's.

Rainy stroked Jennifer's head, not much larger than a lemon; the Yorkie whined soft as a baby bird's whistle. Trembling, she rolled her brown eyes pleadingly and licked Rainy's hand. "She looks just like Azure," Rainy said lovingly, sputtering gently in her sideways lisp.

"Want to come inside for some cookies and milk? I'm really glad you girls are here. Miss Grimsby, you should see what we did to fix up Junior's den."

"Thanks, Mrs. Gallette; cookies and milk sound delicious. Azure, Rainy, should we each carry a bag?"

"Call me Dolly," our new foster mother said. "Come in; come in and make yourselves at home."

The first thing Dolly had wanted to do was show us the house while Miss Grimsby was there. Inside the front door was a scent of coffee, Pine-Sol, lemon Jean Naté bath powder, and very faintly, cigarette smoke, the combination of which was the scent of Dolly herself. After whispering with the social worker she asked us to leave our black plastic garbage bags of clothes that smelled like Mrs. Kukonen's house outside on the front deck. Later she would have Junior carry them to the basement, where she helped us sort things out.

Dolly first took us on a tour, which for a small two-bedroom house took some time. She had fixed up Vernon Junior's bedroom for us, and he had moved into what she called the den ("used to be the sewing room"), which was actually the pantry next to the kitchen. The tiny space had a window with a built-in counter underneath and one wall of shallow shelves and cabinets that she had used to store her sewing scissors, thread, and patterns; unwearable cotton dresses, skirts, and shirts from the rag bin at Used-a-Bit, which Dolly collected for her hobby of making patchwork quilts for the Golden Manor nursing home; receipts and warranties for everything they bought; Christmas tree ornaments and lights; tools; and canned goods.

Across from the cabinets there had been space for a wooden work table, pole lamp, and chair; that is where Dolly had sat as she sewed, listening to the radio on the pantry counter. Just for Rainy and me they had emptied the sewing room of everything, moved Vernon Junior's clothes and books to the cabinets, and bought a new single bed for Junior to sleep in. The small bed didn't have a headboard, which would have extended the length of the bed into the doorway and made closing the door impossible.

"It was surprising how everything fit in here," Dolly said, showing Miss Grimsby the room. "The door opens out to the kitchen, which makes all the difference; Vernon can pull it closed when he wants to be by himself. He's real happy that the girls can have the bedroom and the double bed."

"It is cozy, isn't it? And so much storage room in those cabinets," said Miss Grimsby.

"See how his books line up so nice on the counter?" asked Dolly. "And Vernon's clothes all fit inside the cupboard doors." She opened one, showcasing two stacks of men's white underwear and one of white handkerchiefs folded into precise, squared off towers. I looked away, embarrassed for Vernon Junior, who I hadn't met but now knew where he kept his underwear.

"So here's my room—nothing much here to see." Dolly's bedroom was large, with a quilt-covered ("I made that myself; it's a sunbonnet girls pattern") double bed, the sewing table and chair, and a low dresser covered with bottles of lotion and cologne, cans of hairspray, and small framed photographs. On the floor next to the dresser was a small pink dog bed, which Jennifer jumped onto, yapping.

"No barking!" Dolly whispered loudly, placing an index finger on her own nose. "See? You know what this means." Jennifer silenced. "Good girl. Azure, would you like to give her a reward?" Dolly took a dog treat from her shirt pocket and held it out to me. I fed it to Jennifer, who ate it neatly and then looked beseechingly at Rain.

"Oh, all right." Dolly handed a dog treat to Rain, who fed it to Jennifer. The Yorkie settled into her padded fleecy pallet and resting her chin on her paws sighed happily.

"So here's your room, girls—I kept the door shut so that you can get a good look all at once! What do you think?" Dolly grandly opened the door across the hall from her own bedroom and waved us inside. "It's all pink and purple," she said unnecessarily.

I had never seen anything as beautiful as that room, with its lavender walls, white curtains, and pink-and-purple-flowered bedspread. The closet, empty except for an extra set of sheets and pillowcases, a dozen pink plastic hangers, and a white clothes basket, had also been painted lavender. On either side of the bed was a small table and a lamp with a pink shade. The battered-looking bureau was covered by a pink hand towel ("It's a little scarred up") and two pink plastic bins, each with a new toothbrush, one purple and one pink.

We would have stayed in that pretty bedroom, Rainy and I, but Dolly wanted us and especially Miss Grimsby to see the rest of the house. So we looked next in the basement, where Vernon Junior kept his weight bench next to the washer and dryer, and then at the backyard and in the garage. Everything was tidy and clean, which we would later find didn't come naturally to Dolly, although it did to Junior.

We ended up in the sparkly clean (for the day) kitchen dunking Oreos into mugs of milk while listening to Dolly and Miss Grimsby talk about school, and the ICWA worker from the reservation who would be in touch to make a home visit within a month.

"So is Indian Child Welfare going to be a lot different from the County?" Dolly asked, a little timidly. "I mean, do they come in and inspect the house? Do they care that Vernon sleeps in the pantry, or that the girls have to share a bed?"

"Indian Child Welfare is so new to me; I don't really know much about it at all, just that the reservation decides where children will be placed and that being placed with relatives is a priority with them. The Mozhay Point social worker will be working with the County services, and Azure and Rainfall are still on my caseload—so I might be assigned to visit you, but I will always let you know."

"How old is Vernon Junior?" Rain whispered to me.

"Your house is nice, Mrs. Gallette, and the County would be fine with everything about it, so I can't imagine that ICWA wouldn't be. And you and Vernon requested this. The girls have been returned to their family and tribe. That is the reason for ICWA in the first place. I can't speak for ICWA or the County, of course, but I cannot imagine that they would have any problem at all with your lovely home. Really, I mean that."

Returned to our family and tribe? Would we eventually be returned to Loretta?

"Your cousin Vernon, he's a grown-up." said Dolly, answering Rain. "You can just call him Junior; that's what everybody calls him."

"Where is he?" I asked.

"He's on his way to a meeting; he goes a couple of times a week. Then he'll go to work; he works nights, so you'll see him in the morning."

The County had given Sammy permission to get us a whole week off from school. This would give us time to get used to a new house, and for Dolly and cousin Vernon—no, everybody called him Junior, remember—to get used to us as well. Junior worked nights at the hospital where he was the east wing security guard; he walked floors from eleven to seven, and when people died during the night he brought their bodies to the morgue on wheeled stretchers, all by himself in the basement. "Is it scary?" Rain asked him one time. Junior paused, as was his way, giving thought before he answered. "No-o-o, there's nothing to be scared of; they're just these poor people who couldn't go on living." He would get home early in the morning, around the time we would be leaving for school, dog-tired and wanting a warm milk that Dolly got for him before he had breakfast and then went to bed for the day. He liked to read and took us to the library every other Tuesday night after supper, when Dolly was at her canasta club.

Except for those Tuesday nights at the library we didn't see much of Junior, who slept during the days and spent the evenings before work reading the newspaper; watching TV; or lifting, carrying, or moving furniture for Dolly, who had trouble with her back sometimes but liked rearranging furniture. Twice a week he went to his meetings, which we eventually learned were for AA, Alcoholics Anonymous. On evenings and weekends when he wasn't busy doing all that, he was busy driving all of us, Dolly, Rain, and me, wherever we wanted to go. Heavy and dark-skinned with a smile that creased his cheeks, Junior was a quiet man who seemed content to let Dolly do most of the talking, who didn't say much, and seemed would rather listen than speak. He was the reason for our removal from Mrs. Kukonen's, Dolly told us, and our new placement with our family, though we were too shy to ask what that meant exactly.

"The only thing is, you have to remember not to make a lot of noise around Junior," Dolly told us, "on account of him being in Vietnam when he was in the Army, and he gets a little nervous sometimes. When he does, he just ups and leaves, goes walking. He's not mad or anything, but just remember to not make a lot of noise around him."

The first Saturday at Dolly's, Junior got up at 10 o'clock, giving up half a day's sleep to drive us all over town, waiting in the car reading and listening to the radio while Dolly took us looking for new school clothes. At Kmart we got underwear and socks; at JCPenney, jeans, sweaters, jackets, and shoes; and at Snyder Drug, colored ponytail elastics and barrettes, all picked out by Dolly, who as she said, never did get her own baby girl and really loved all these pretty things, and that they never made cute stuff for boys when Junior was little. At a shop downtown, mysteriously called Northern Supplies, Dolly bought a box of hospital pads for Rainy's side of the bed, disposable ones that could be thrown out.

In the week we had off before we started back to school we spent a lot of time doing things around the house, to "get used to the place," as Dolly put it. Much of this involved moving things around, which was one of Dolly's favorite things to do and which, as she also put it, "kept things from getting dusty." We reordered the books on the bookshelf in the front room, emptied the china cabinet in the dining room, and rearranged the knickknacks and dishes. We put our new clothes away in the dresser drawers and in the closet. We emptied our plastic garbage bags of clothing and school papers out on Junior's work table in the basement, and to our surprise, at the bottom of one was a naked Barbie doll wadded into a pair of snow pants, overlooked somehow by Mrs. Kukonen. Dolly let us give Barbie a bubble bath in the stationary tub while she put a load of light-colored clothes into the washing machine, adding a handful of baking soda for the mustiness. We helped hang the clean laundry on the clothesline in the backyard, which aired things out a little more, then sorted what we wanted to keep, what would make good cleaning rags, and what would be given away. Which wasn't much.

"We don't want to palm any crap off on poor people," was how Dolly put it. "Plenty of people do that, which is a shitty thing to do to them, pardon my French."

We sat Barbie between our toothbrush boxes on the dresser, clothed in a washcloth with some bias tape from Dolly's sewing box wrapped around the waist and tied in a bow. Dolly thought having Barbie sit around bare-naked would be vulgar and said she would help us sew something for her to wear later on, after things got settled a little more.

Midafternoons we watched *General Hospital* with Dolly, and by Wednesday I felt easy enough around her, once the program was over, to ask her about people in the framed pictures on the walls and on top of the bookshelf next to the television. She placed each in our hands as she told us about them, replacing each one carefully after we had had time to look at them.

The snapshot in the cardboard frame on the bookshelf of

a serious-looking blonde teenage Dolly had been taken by her mother after church one day in Minneapolis; sixteen-year-old Dolly squinted, her glasses held in her hand and half-hidden against the side of her skirt.

In the small silver frame a woman in a flowered hat held a frilly, lacy bundle of blanket and baptism dress; a baby's surprised-looking face peeked out of the mass of ruffles at the woman, whose large lipsticked mouth was puckered in a kissing shape. Next to her a wrinkled, bald man grinned happily at the camera. "Vernon Junior with his godparents," Dolly explained. "Winnie and Ingrum, such nice people. A long time ago, I guess." She dusted the glass, lightly, with her sweatshirt sleeve.

Above the bookshelf hung Junior's high school graduation picture and next to it his Army picture, taken before he went overseas. Between them in an 8x10 with a scrolled brass frame was a blurry enlargement of a snapshot, a small boy in coveralls seated on porch steps next to a woman in a floral-patterned housedress. Her face, in profile, looked down tenderly at the little boy whose head rested lovingly against her elbow, oblivious to the camera. "That's Junior with his grandma, Maggie; she is your grandma, too—your great-grandmother. She died when he was little, not long after this picture."

"Would you like to see a picture of Vernon Senior?" Dolly asked. "Azure, if you'll go into my bedroom, you'll see it's on the table next to my bed. Bring it out here, would you?"

Winnie and Ingrum again, this time flanking a skinny, happy teenage boy wearing baggy, high-waisted pants and a ribbed undershirt—Winnie on one side with an arm around the boy's neck, Ingrum on the other with an arm around the boy's waist. "I took this one," Dolly said. "Just before he went in the Army. He went missing overseas; we never saw him again. Vernon Junior never saw his father at all." She lay the picture on her lap. "This was at the bowling alley, the Palace Bowl; that's where Vernon and his cousin Sam were working." She took in a deep breath; I waited for her to expel it in a sigh, but instead she coughed into her sweater sleeve and swiped at her nose with her shirttail.

"And now here we are, here we are—be careful putting the picture back on the bedside table, will you? And I have another picture to show you; I was going to get it enlarged and framed before you got here, but we were so excited about fixing up your room that I forgot." Dolly walked back to Junior's room, where we heard her open and close a cupboard door. When she came back into the front room she was carrying a small clear plastic envelope.

"Your auntie Artense gave this to Junior when he was looking for you. It's a picture of her and your mother, Loretta, when they were about five years old; Artense says it's from the photo booth in the old Woolworth's downtown."

The wallet-sized black-and-white photograph was of two girls, each with an arm around the other's shoulders. Both were wearing kerchiefs tied under the chin; both had short, thick bangs; one girl smiled open-mouthed, innocently unaware of her pointy eye teeth; the other looked solemnly into the camera lens.

"That's Loretta, the smiley girl; the other is her cousin, your auntie Artense."

Rain and I looked closely at the photo.

"She's excited," said Rain, touching the plastic over our mother's little-girl face with her fingertips.

"Yes, she was always an excited, active little girl whenever I saw her," Dolly answered. "They had a lot of fun together, Artense and Loretta; Artense says this picture was from when Loretta was visiting and Patsy took them downtown. There would be three more of these; you went in this little booth and put in a quarter, and the camera flashed four times, then a couple of minutes later it spit out a strip of four pictures. People cut them apart, see? This one is cut crooked at the bottom, looks like somebody used nail scissors."

Rain pointed at Artense. "Was she mad?"

"Nooooo . . . That's just the way Artense is; kind of a worrier, I guess."

"They look like sisters, like us," I said, wondering if my words had any truth to them.

Dolly tucked the plastic-sleeved photo into the corner of Junior's baptism picture. "We'll take it to First Photo this week and get it enlarged, and we'll get a nice frame and put it above the bookshelf right next to the picture of Junior and Maggie."

On Friday of the week we had off to get ready for school, Dolly took us to the Academy of Hair Design for haircuts and perms. My beauty-school girl fixed mine just like the social worker's: it looked like shiny ribbons curling in spirals almost all the way down to my shoulder blades. I loved it.

Rainy's hairdo took a lot longer. Dolly and I read magazines — Dolly going outside twice for a cigarette — until Rain came out with shining eyes and a permanent that wasn't like mine at all. A two-inch-high oval of tightly curled, somewhat frizzy hair covered the crown of her head, joined at the back to a second oval that extended to the nape of her neck; the sides were plastered upwards with hair gel that had been sprinkled with silver glitter. It was called a Mohawk, Rain told us excitedly, and was the newest style. Her beauty-school girl smiled proudly.

Holy cow, Dolly whispered to herself, but "My, how fancy!" she said aloud.

Our beauty-school students beamed. "We have to get the manager here to check the cuts and the perms," my student said.

"Miss Donna! We're ready for a check!" called Rain's student.

The manager, who inspected and measured the cut and perm, pronounced both to be perfect. "Excellent work, both of you."

Dolly cleared her throat. "Are you girls going to show them how they get their hair this way when they're getting ready for school?" They were. "Well, why don't you do that while I talk to your teacher, here."

Dolly whispered to the beauty-school manager that she was going to have to do something else with Rainy's head. She couldn't let her out of the house with a hairdo that not only made her look like a chippie, but how in the world would she ever get a hairbrush through it? She'd spent all that money so we'd look nice for school, not so Rainy would stand out like a wild . . . wild . . . Dolly searching for the right word.

"Well, the cut *is* called a Mohawk; that's the style."

"See, what I am saying here is that she doesn't have it easy, because she's a little slow," she explained in a more urgent whisper almost directly into the manager's ear. "We're trying to make her look like she'll fit in."

"She needs to be able to fix her hair, herself, for school in the morning," she said loudly to the eavesdropping beauty-school student, who had become tearful. "It's not that you didn't do a good job; it just needs to be a little easier to fix for every day. She can wear it this fancy way for church, maybe."

Which is how Rain ended up with this hairdo that could be plaited right down to her scalp and down the back of her skull into a French braid. Gently, Rain's student coaxed the ovals of curls into a thick herringbone shape that she secured at the bottom with a silver elastic band.

"Very nice, Caroline," said the manager. "Let her see the back."

Caroline spun Rain's chair around and gave her a mirror, helping her to position it. "Do you like it?" She smiled nervously.

"It's so pretty," said Rain. "And I look so tall."

I could tell that Rain's hairdo was still a little untamed for Dolly's taste, but the manager said that Rain's hair would train itself and calm down before too long. In the meantime, Caroline would show Dolly and me how to fix a French braid at home. We watched her take the plait apart and section her hair with a wide-toothed comb, then with her fingers weave Rain's hair down the back of her head from the crown to the bottom, past the nape of her neck, securing the end again with a silver elastic band.

"Want to try it?" Miss Donna asked Dolly, who after two tries that only tangled Rain's hair into knots that had to be combed out by the manager, gave up.

"Ow," said Rainy, rubbing her head.

"How about your other girl? Want to give it a try, honey?"

I was so afraid of getting my hands stuck in Rain's perm and hurting her that my braid came out loose and sloppy, but the manager said that I had the hang of it.

"They can practice this at home," she said to Dolly. "They can play beauty salon with each other's hair. Here," she said to me, "try it one more time. I'll watch."

"I can do it," said Rainy, loosening her braid. Holding the silver elastic band in her teeth she wide-combed the curls and put down the comb, then touched her head with her fingertips, each an inch apart, one hand above each ear. Without looking at the mirror and without the comb, she French-braided her own hair by feel, walking her fingers down the back of her head and lifting each section that she had tapped with her fingertips, winding the few inches of hair left at the bottom with the silver elastic band into a figure-eight.

"Well," said Dolly, "how in the world did you do that?"

"I don't know, I just did."

At the cash register Dolly picked up bottles of shampoo, conditioner, and detangler and a wide-toothed comb, and she let us each choose a little jar of lip gloss from a bowl on the counter. "Give both of those beauty students a nice tip, will you," she said to the manager as she wrote a check. Then Dolly stepped back and looked us up and down.

"You are the most beautiful girls I ever saw," she said.

· · ·

The Saturday before we started school, Junior took us to a sobriety powwow. I didn't think we'd ever gone to a powwow before and asked Dolly if we had to go—she told us we had been to powwows when we were little and might remember about them once we got there. We would probably even see people we knew.

I swallowed, then cleared my throat. "I can't think of anybody we would know?" I put it as a meek-sounding question, but it was taking a chance: Mrs. Kukonen would have cracked me across the ear, but in the week and a half we had been at Dolly's she hadn't shown any sign of hitting us.

This was Dolly's opportunity to tell us that our mother would be there, if she was going to be anywhere, but she didn't say anything about Loretta at all.

"Well, they know you," was all she said.

"Can't we stay here with you?" This from Rainy.

"Can you come with?" Me.

"I'm going with my friend Rose first; you haven't met her yet, but we do daywork together—we have a job today at the American Legion, but if we don't get out of there too late, I hope I can make it there in time for the feast. Sis tries to get up to Chris Jensen, the nursing home, to visit her mother's friend Lisette on Saturdays, and she'll drop me off at the Coppertop when we get the job finished." This was the First Methodist Church at the top of the hill, with the copper roof.

"Do you know what time?"

"I don't know—just don't worry; it will be fine. You'll have fun. Do it for Junior."

She fussed a little as we got dressed, had me take off my blouse so that she could iron the front and put a crease into the sleeves, and then changed the ribbon at the bottom of Rainy's braid to a new one, green to match her eyes. She shot one short burst of hair-spray onto the top of Rain's head and lightly smoothed any bits of permed curls sticking out from the braid.

"You look nice," she said, circling to look us over from all sides. "Prettiest girls there."

Outside, a car honked twice, lightly. Dolly waved out the door, "Coming, Sis!" and picked up a plastic laundry basket of cleaning supplies. "Will you carry the bag of dust rags?" she asked. I handed the rags to Rainy and lifted one side of the laundry basket.

As we placed the laundry basket and bag of rags into the back seat of the car, Sis—who evidently was also Rose and had watched us as we walked from the porch and all the way down to the curb—looked closely at our faces.

"Azure Sky and Rainfall Dawn," she said. "How do you like it at your new house?"

"Good."

"Nice."

Her smile was a cheery mouthful of crooked teeth. "I bet you do; I saw your room when Dolly and Junior were fixing it up, all that pink and purple. Have fun at the powwow!"

They drove off, Dolly waving, and Rainy and I went back into the house to wait for Junior, me trying but unable to remember anything at all about powwows.

In the years since that afternoon at the Methodist church Rain and I have been to many powwows; we have risen with the other spectators for the flag bearers and the dancers, for the entrance of the dancers into the circle, for the invocation, for the Veterans dance, and for the honoring and intertribal dances. As adults we became traditional dancers, my sister and me, plain and prayerful in the simple dresses we sewed for ourselves, and now, older, each time that we line up for Grand Entry we stand in our right and proper place according to the order of age that every year places us closer to the beginning of the lineup. In front of us are the women traditional dancers in buckskin dresses; following, we in ribbon-trimmed calico match our steps to theirs as we enter the circle, as the jingle and fancy shawl dancers do theirs to ours. Each time, whether I am dancing or watching from the side, my heart lifts with happiness and gratitude at being a part of this, but I cherish the early memory of the sobriety powwow at the Coppertop church the most dearly. It was there that Auntie Girlie told Rain and me that we look like our mother—her gift to Loretta and to us that acknowledged and clarified our right and proper place in the LaForce and Gallette families, and in the world, as surely as the order of women dancers at Grand Entry.

But on that day when I was thirteen and Rain fourteen, the two of us in the back seat of Junior's car looking out the windows at the houses and stores lined up along the streets of Duluth, we felt out of place and afraid. And thankful for Junior, who was all we had.

At the church parking lot a man on foot approached the car, lurching heavily to the left with each step. Junior lifted one hand in greeting and opened his window; the man peered into the car. "Vernon Gallette, sir!" removing his stocking hat and bowing deeply, hat swept in a generous half-circle by one hand. "Ain't seen you in two days—what's the good word?" He and Junior shook hands raised palm to palm, and the man set the hat back on his head, where it perched like a raggy gray butterfly.

"Brought somebody with me." Vernon opened the back door. "Come out, you girls, and meet a friend of mine. Howard Dulebohn, this is Rainfall and Azure."

"Rainfall. Azure. Loretta's daughters, hey." Howard nodded; his hat jumped forward to just over his left eye. "Happy to meet you."

"Hi," Rain answered nervously.

"Happy to meet you, too," I mumbled.

"Do you need any help carrying anything?"

Dolly had made Rice Krispie bars for the feast and had stacked them onto two doubled paper plates that she covered with plastic wrap. She told us to bring them directly to the kitchen from the car, to keep them clean, not set them on the floor of the car, not lift the plastic, and especially not let any little kids at them, because who knows when they last washed their hands. Although Howard wasn't a little kid, his hands didn't look too clean, and the paper plates were so white.

"No; thank you, though; we're okay," I answered.

We walked in a little procession toward the doors of the Coppertop church basement, Junior and Howard in front and Rainy and I in back, walking so close to one another that I bumped her shoulder with mine. "Be careful of the Rice Krispie bars," she said.

"We'd better not walk so fast." We slowed our steps, which was enough to delay our entrance by several seconds.

We left Junior and Howard at the sign-in table to enter all of our names for the door prize drawing and found the kitchen, crowded with cooks and helpers. From somewhere near the sink a woman called out, "What have you got there? Bars? You can put them on the counter by the window."

Outside the kitchen we could hear drumming and singing; at the end of the wide hallway the auditorium doors were wide open, and between us and the powwow, dancers were standing in line against the wall. One of them, a woman in a fringed buckskin dress, waved a feathered fan back and forth across her face and chest. She smiled.

"Getting warm in here, huh? Are you girls looking for somebody?"

"Umm . . . the bathroom?"

"Right behind you!" And so it was, *Ladies* stenciled in script under the silhouette of a colonial woman in a wide-skirted dress.

She was there in the ladies' room, the light coming in from the window she faced bright yet diffused to a glow by the white of the nylon curtains, so that she was to us a hazy figure in blue dancing with her back to us. Her shawl, pinned to her shoulders and wrists, spread as she parted the curtains and opened the window, the breeze blowing the fringe from her shawl and her smoky exhalation back towards us as we watched, riveted and breathless. She bent, leaning out the window and calling to someone outside.

My heart pounded and I couldn't speak. Loretta. I was certain that I would recognize her anywhere, but would she recognize us? She dipped, rose, leaned on her elbows as she spoke through the window to a shadow that moved across the sunlit white curtains, oblivious to Rain and me as we went to the bathroom, flushed the toilets, washed our hands. Was she a ghost?

We took the little jars of lip gloss from our jeans pockets and applied the pink goo to our carefully pooched-out lips, all the time watching the ghost behind our shoulders in the mirror, who waved her hands towards the open window; the semi-sheer curtains stirred in the moving air, rippling the shadow; a male ghost voice returned her murmur. She laughed; the shadow silenced and vanished.

I cleared my throat. "Hi," I said. She jumped slightly and turned, not Loretta at all but a girl my age, taller than Rain but shorter than me, dressed in a blue satin powwow dress with a matching shawl. Her shiny slicked-back hair was parted straight down the center of her head and plaited into two skinny braids the length and shape of chocolate licorice Twizzlers, bound at her ears with beaded hair ties shaped like deep pink roses. The wide belt around her waist matched the hair ties, as did the beaded vamps on her new-looking white moccasins. She took a last drag on her cigarette and parted the curtains, exhaling the fogginess of the end of her smoke out the open window. She raised one eyebrow, licked her thumb and fore-finger, and pinched the butt, then with an overhand toss pitched it out the window, a good shot.

It was only then that she looked at us directly and coolly. "Hi," she said back in a gravelly voice. "Are you looking for a place to change? The dressing room is on the other side of the building, the

Sunday school nursery room. Nobody will care if you change in here, though."

"No . . ." Suddenly I wished for nothing more than a satin dance outfit with a beaded belt and matching hair ties and moccasins.

"We're here with our cousin, Junior Gallette," said Rain.

The girl stared, her narrow eyes widening, taking in Rain's and my new hairdos and outfits. And stared some more. "Oh, yeah?" she asked. "I like your hair," she said. "Both of you."

Out in the hallway several boys were horsing around at a drinking fountain, shoving and knocking into each other and the wall. "Hey, Crystal!" one called. "Got a cigarette?" Another bumped against a boy who was drinking from the water spout. "Hey, watch it!" The chunky boy wiped his mouth on the back of his hand and smiled at Rainy, then turned his back to us, bending to drink again, his backside sticking out. Another boy called, "Freddie-Boy wants to show you something!" and pulled the boy's sweatpants down to his knees and exposed his underwear, grayed and baggy, with a rip at the waistband.

"Not funny, asshole!" the boy pulled his pants up and ran away down the hall and out the doors to the parking lot.

"Grow up, Nolie; you are so pathetic." Crystal visibly stuck her nose in the air; Rain and I did the same, and the three of us walked away with dignity and contempt for such juvenile behavior, me swinging my permed head so that my ribbon curls bounced with my version of buzz-off-come-hither huffiness.

"Want to sit together? I'm here with my mom and her friend, and a bunch of relatives. Do you want to dance at intertribal? You can dance with me if you want."

Nothing prepared me for the sight of a powwow, and yet it didn't seem unfamiliar at all. In the center of the room, a half-dozen men sat on metal folding chairs around a drum, a blanket spread beneath it. The song was led first by one man, then as the others chimed in their voices were in unison, as was their striking of the drum with sticks wrapped on the ends with sheepskin. The lead singer cupped a hand to his left ear, listening to himself as he sang; another picked a glass of water from the floor next to his chair and took a sip, then resumed singing. Several people danced clockwise around the drum: two girls dressed in satin dresses like Crystal's, one pink and one red, matched steps; one shortened her steps while the other lengthened hers, then they did the opposite and once again matched steps; an old man in a black velvet beaded vest and baggy work pants double-stomped heavily, bent slightly forward at the waist; several small children, some in powwow clothing and some in everyday jeans and T-shirts, followed the other dancers, copying their steps. Two rows of folding chairs had been arranged around three of the four walls; Junior and Howard had joined the crowd milling at the doorway of the fourth wall. Timid, Rain and I paused in front of Junior; to our surprise he spoke to all of us.

"So you found somebody you know," he said. Then, to Crystal, "Do you ever look nice."

"Can they sit with us?" Crystal asked. "My mom and them are right over there." She indicated the direction with a slight sharp point of her chin.

"Sure; you girls have fun; I'll come over in a while to say hello."

Crystal led us toward a group of people sitting on folding chairs; the woman second from the end spoke into the ear of the elderly woman on the end, who was enthroned in a high-backed cushioned lawn chair that must have been brought especially for her comfort. "That's Auntie Beryl, and that really old lady is Auntie Girlie — come on, they see us. Watch out what you say to my mom; she is always on my case and looking for something to give me crap about. Gawd, she made these braids so tight." Crystal wiggled her hair ties to loosen them.

To our surprise Beryl took our hands, Rain's and mine.

"Aneen. I am happy to see youse; my, you've grown into

beautiful young women." She shook our hands and then let go to pat her hair, a black beehive that towered three inches over her head, feeling for the four front-facing teased-in loops of hair that we would later learn she called "flirt curls."

"Girlie, these are Loretta's girls, Azure Sky and Rainfall Dawn." Beryl spoke in the direction of the old woman in the cushioned lawn chair, who grasped the arms of the chair with her long, claw-like hands and sat upright. A crocheted granny-square afghan was draped over her skinny-bones body from her knees to her collarbone. Above her long, crepey neck her bright white hair was lightly twisted into a little knot at the top of her head; fine strands that had worked themselves out of the knot framed her round, nearly unlined face in an eerily moving halo. On her feet, which stuck out below the edge of the afghan, were beaded moccasins and pink-striped socks. I thought that given the distance between her head and her toes she must be an unusually tall woman, and she was so thin that the afghan could just as well have been empty. She waggled her feet back and forth, the cut-glass beaded flowers on her moccasins catching light and sparkling under the fluorescent fixtures overhead. Her eyes were oddly cloudy; as she turned them toward us they glittered, specks of appearing and disappearing points of light, smaller even than those from the individuals beads that made up the roses above her toes. The effect was, to me, magical; she might have been a good witch or a fairy.

Beryl placed Rain's and my hands into those of the magical old woman, who bent her head into our little half-circle.

"Loretta's girls? Oh, I was hoping that you would be here." The old woman (Girlie or Auntie Girlie? Was she a relative?) ran her thumb gently across the backs of my and Rain's hands, her peculiarly sparkling eyes on something far past the space between our shoulders. Her gaze drifted across our faces, then focused again on something beyond the two girls presented to her in that Methodist church auditorium. "You look like your mother, both of you."

4

AUNTIE GIRLIE

It was the trachoma. The kids at the Harrod Indian School didn't know the name for it and just called it "the eye disease," and somebody brought it to Harrod the year I was sixteen; I suppose it doesn't matter how it got there. That was a long time ago, when there were still people alive who knew me as Angeline Robineau; I was one of the bigger girls who were helping take care of the little children, who all called me Miss Angeline. The eye disease spread like wildfire in that dormitory; I got it the worst, and it was sure weeks and weeks of misery. Once the swelling went down and my eyelids turned themselves back to the outside, I began to see again in a fashion, through those sore, swollen slits that got a little bigger every day as they healed.

Although I am not completely blind, since then I have viewed the world through the scars left on my corneas, as if everything out there is on the other side of a rain-spattered window, wavy and distorted. The haze of distance is clearer than what is close, and light and darkness play tricks on what is already for an old woman a landscape of layers of past and present, of people and events that passed across my line of vision both before the eye disease and ever since.

But I have learned to compensate for what I cannot see clearly and was able to recognize Crystal as she emerged from the moving blur of people milling around the auditorium; she was at first a glow of blue and rose pink satin that caught and reflected the sun shining in through the bank of windows, or perhaps it was the fluorescent lights overhead. I recognized her voice—since she began to talk, which if I remember correctly was a little late for her age, her voice has reminded me of a mallard's—and I heard Crystal complaining about her mother, my niece Margie. As she walked closer to the rows of folding chairs where Beryl, Margie, and the other La-Forces were waiting for Grand Entry to begin (Beryl always arrived at powwows early in order to claim a dozen seats near an exit as she was afraid of a fire), I could see that she was with two other girls.

"Oh, my, will you look at this." Beryl sounded a little breathy. "Those must be Loretta's girls—see, they were just talking with Junior and Howard. Crystal is bringing them over here. Oh, my, my . . . Did you ever think we would see those three babies together again?"

"They look so shy," said Margie. "We have to make sure they have a place to sit here with us—Crystal's going to have to leave to line up." She placed her purse and jacket on two more chairs in the first row. "Uncle Noel, save these chairs, all right?" she asked.

"He doesn't hear you." Beryl clucked her tongue and raised her voice. "Noel! Save those two chairs, will you?"

Exaggerating, Noel held one hand to the side of his head like an ear trumpet. "Wegonen? What's that, niwiiw ikwe? Shave those two hairs?"

Beryl rolled her eyes. "I married a comedian."

Margie snickered. "Migwech, Uncle."

Beryl placed two soft, young hands, into mine and introduced us. "Loretta's girls? Oh, I was hoping that you would be here." One girl was taller than the other and had beautiful hair, like sun shining on a dark cloud; the smaller girl, who bent close, closer to my face, had light eyes. How I wished that I could see their faces clearly. "You look like your mother, both of you."

"Are you ready?" Margie walked all around Crystal, straightening her shawl. "Are her hair ties even?" she asked Beryl, prodding at Crystal's rose hair ties, which she thought were sliding down her skinny braids.

Beryl tilted her head, squinting. "Margie, I think the left side is a little lower than the right."

"Look at me, Crystal." Margie and Crystal stood face to face, Margie measuring the planes of her daughter's cheekbones and the height of the slipping hair ties with her eyes. If Crystal's eyes had been larger and rounder, her nose shorter and ever so slightly upturned, and her complexion closer to a peach tone, she and her mother would have looked like twins; as it was they looked like sisters, the younger one impatient and the prettier one worried.

Tightening one rose hair tie and loosening the other, Margie was close enough to smell what I had been able to smell, cigarette. She grew closer, kissed her daughter's cheek, and inhaled deeply, picked up Crystal's hand, and sniffed, wrinkled her nose at the smell. "Oh, Crystal."

Beryl too sniffed in Crystal's direction. A smoker herself, she wouldn't have been able to smell the cigarette. I sensed movement, heard the fumbling sounds of Beryl's hand checking in her purse for her pack of Camels, finding it, counting by touch how many remained in the pack. Not that she would ever tell on Crystal, I knew.

Crystal returned her mother's reproachful look with a defiant one. "Got to go get in line; warm-ups are about done. See you after." Crystal waved a hand towards my eyes. "Nagach, Auntie Girlie; webaa." She muttered towards Loretta's girls, "Don't let her boss you around," and was gone.

AZURE SKY

"What is Dolly up to today?" asked Beryl. "She gonna get to the powwow?"

"She's doing daywork with her friend Rose."

"Oh, a cleaning job. Is this their Saturday at the Legion? That's a good one."

"Five minutes to Grand Entry!" the voice boomed statically from a microphone that was hooked into a portable speaker. "This is your emcee speaking! Five minutes! Grand Entry will begin at one o'clock, and that's one o'clock sharp, not Indian time!" Several people laughed. "Dancers are lining up in the hall; all you dancers take your places. Five minutes to Grand Entry! . . . Make that four!"

The warm-up song ended, the singers rose, stretched; the handful of dancers warming up left the hall. Nolie, his demeanor changed from what it had been at the drinking fountain, approached the drum, offering a small bowl to the lead singer, a white-haired older man.

"Aniin, Zho Wash," Nolie said deferentially. "Here's some butterscotch candy and some cough drops from the cooks. I'm going to bring you a pitcher of water and some cups, too."

"Migwech," the older man answered.

"Gaye giin." Nolie lingered.

"Giin dash; are you going to sing with us today, you and Duane? How about young Freddie-Boy; he going to sing with us, too?"

"Sure." Nolie had a nice smile, I thought, even though he was juvenile as Crystal had said. "We been practicing that intertribal."

AUNTIE GIRLIE

"Come a little closer so I can see you, Azure Sky and Rainfall Dawn," I said, pulling the half-circle of our joined hands closer. The smaller girl crooked her arm into that of the taller. "Noel, why don't you lift those chairs from over there so they can sit by me. You girls look like your mother," I said, thinking that they would like my saying that but really not seeing Loretta in them at all. Who I was thinking of, and who I saw, were my mother and her sister, Maggie and Helen, both long gone from this world but always so close — like these two girls, Maggie's granddaughters, were to me now.

In late spring of the year before trachoma arrived at Harrod,

Mother had sent money for train fares to the superintendent so that me and my brothers Sonny and George could go live with her in Duluth for the summer at the house on Garfield Avenue, down by the grain elevators and scrap yard. We had all lived up north in Mozhay Point before, in Mother's family's allotment house at Sweetgrass, from the time we were born until we were sent away, one by one, to the Indian school. That year before the eye disease only our two littlest brothers, Vernon and Jerome, whom we called Giizis and Biik, were still at home. Mother had moved to Duluth a few years before that, when we older children were away at Indian school and Giizis and Biik were still in diapers; she left my father, Andre—escaped, really. I can't speak to the circumstances involved in Louis Gallette's being the father of the little boys; they were born during one of those periods of time that Andre had abandoned us. He had been gone for years, but Andre begged her to let him come back, and then once she gave in, he reminded her of it constantly, getting angrier and angrier and slapping her around. It got worse when George, Sonny, and me were away at school, so bad that, as Auntie Helen told me, Maggie's leaving and taking the little boys with her from her family's allotment house at Sweetgrass down to Duluth might have saved her life—and Giizis and Biik's, too.

When Mother got to Duluth with Giizis and Biik, the three of them moved in with her older sister Helen, who was having a rough time and needed some help. Mother found a job at the mattress factory and then they moved into the Garfield Avenue house, where they were visited regularly: by people from Mozhay, sometimes for weeks at a time; by Andre, who for part of the summers took Sonny and George to help in his Indian store up near Mesabi or on the road to sell beadwork and baskets to tourists and travelers from his truck; and by Biik and Giizis's father, and Maggie's true love, Louis.

It is complicated, the story of Mother and her two husbands, the first by Catholic marriage in a ceremony performed by the priest at the mission church in Mozhay Point, and the second by the Indian way, what was called in those times "common law." Mother's life was not an easy one, and Andre, who had less right than anyone to fault her for anything, made it harder for her and everyone else involved, including me, the oldest daughter who did what I could to help, which wasn't enough, and outlived them all: Mother, Auntie Helen, Andre, Louis, Sonny, George, Giizis, and Biik. I have sometimes wondered why that is: surely there must be a reason.

You know, being an Elder is made quite a big deal over, and although I am now about the oldest Elder around, I don't think I have done anything to have earned it beyond continuing to breathe longer than other people. Nonetheless, it has come to be part of my everyday life to be acknowledged with honor, and Crystal, spoiled *oshkinikwe* though she be, was raised by her mother to have proper Ojibwe manners and so would bring her newly found cousins, Louis and Maggie's great-granddaughters and my great-grandnieces, to me—the nearly blind, revered *mindimoye* matriarch of the La-Force family. As *mindemoye* it was my place to acknowledge the place of Loretta's daughters, Azure Sky and Rainfall Dawn, *oshki-oshinikwewag*. And so, "You look like your mother," I said as the Grand Entry song began.

Everyone in the auditorium stood: Vernon Junior and Howard, standing in the aisle next to the LaForces, removed their hats and held them over their hearts. I rose too, sore in the knees and hips and wobbly, though I tried to hide it.

"Help your Auntie Girlie," Beryl whispered to tall Azure, who offered me her hand, which I took only to steady myself, bearing my own weight and standing between Azure Sky and Rainfall Dawn, who although they looked nothing like them, reminded me of Maggie and Helen. The blur that was the world to me tilted; I righted it by rubbing my eyes and then folded my hands at my waist, praying a small request to God, and who knows if He ever bothers with these little things or not: for five minutes, just five, to stand, to remain upright between the warmth and youth of the girls who, found, would link the generations before me to the generations after them. My body swayed but I did not fall, and then

Loretta's girls each took one of my elbows, Azure Sky on the left and Rainfall Dawn on the right. Strengthened and steady I stood.

Since the eye disease at Harrod, the epidemic they called it, I have hardly ever cried, even when Maggie died. The disease had dried my eyes so long ago that the rare tears I had shed ever since were small, and so salty and thick that they stung as they formed. Scarce and occasional, most were absorbed back into my sore eyes; those that escaped didn't travel far but dried stiffly on my cheeks. In my experience since Maggie died, crying had only caused more pain. But standing there for Grand Entry, with the four veterans approaching, blurred and wavy, leading the dancers into the powwow circle and with Loretta's girls holding me up, one on each side, their soft damp *oshkinikwe* hands cupped under my dry, coarse-skinned elbows, the tears that rose and pooled in my eyes were plentiful, lenses that both clarified and soothed.

AZURE SKY

As Grand Entry started, Rainy and I stood with Auntie Girlie, one at each elbow, until after the veterans carrying the flags had passed and she asked us to help her sit. Beryl smiled as we settled her into her cushioned lawn chair; another woman asked Rainy to help tuck a pillow under Girlie's knees, and a man handed me one end of a fringed shawl that we wrapped over her shoulders. It seemed to be as Dolly had said, that they all knew who we were. Margie, Crystal's mother, whispered to us explaining the order of the Grand Entry into the powwow circle: behind the veterans and flags came the men's traditional dancers, men's grass dancers, men's fancy; then the women's traditional, followed by the women's jingle dress and fancy dancers.

"The tiny tots, little children, will follow everybody else," she said, her eyes on Crystal, whose arms lightly swung as she kicked athletically to the side, to the front, then spread her arms like wings, dipping first to the left and then to the right. She looked like a blue-bird, I thought, and I felt proud to know her, the beautifully dressed and confident dancer who was also the coolest girl I had ever seen.

"Wow, she's so pretty," said Rain.

Margie nodded modestly, trying to properly contain her pride; her eyes focused on her daughter, glistening with love and admiration. I would have given just about anything to have my mother there to look at me that way, then I thought that Margie in fact looked sad and worried, and I wondered if the shine in her eyes might be tears and if she was close to weeping. Her pained, liquid gaze followed Crystal until she was around the other side of the powwow circle and out of sight.

"And here are the Tiny Tots! Little dancers, closing the powwow circle!" said the announcer through the microphone. "Our future Elders, dancing to an old traditional song of our people, wuh-ho!"

A collective *Awwwww* sounded through the auditorium. Next to me Beryl leaned toward Margie's ear. I shifted my weight and bent to hear her whisper, "Just look at those two little fat girls dancing together, there; aren't they cute?" Her hands clasped at her waist, she beamed lovingly.

The circle completed and the song ended, then the announcer introduced Mr. Dionne, a very old man who said a very long prayer in Ojibwe as we continued to stand (except for Auntie Girlie). A couple of minutes into the prayer Rainy began to fidget; Girlie pulled her gently by the hand to the edge of the lawn chair to sit and placed a shawl-wrapped arm around Rainy's shoulder.

I knew it was the praying that made Rain fidget. While living at Mrs. Kukonen's, we had spent hours twice a week at God's Sinners Saved listening to lengthy holy diatribes of prayers after the Sinners' extemporary confessions and testimonials; at bedtime every night we knelt on the putrid carpet in front of the couch listening to

Mrs. Kukonen angrily snitch to God about how bad we were and then, on cue, begging for His forgiveness. After Mrs. Kukonen had split Rainy's lip, telling her that we were blasphemers who were nothing but fodder for hell, and she put that permanent crimp into the side of Rainy's mouth and smile, I had told myself that if we ever got out of that house, we wouldn't have anything to do with praying again.

Enfolded by Auntie Girlie's shawl-wrapped arm, Rainy had stilled, but with the Sinners' moaning shouts and Mrs. Kukonen's dramatic tattlings and criticisms echoing in my mind, I felt like fidgeting myself. In the folding chairs behind me two of the La-Force children started whispering "Touched you last!" to each other and giggling; their father shushed them and Margie dug a stick of gum out of her pocket, which she tore in half and gave to the children. Across the room an infant began to cry; its mother pulled up the bottom of her shirt, covered the baby's head and her breast with a small blanket, and began to nurse. Mr. Dionne continued the prayer. Some of the older people sat, some dancers shifted their weight from one foot to the other. Auntie Girlie affirmed, "Mmmmm, hmmmmmm" every once in a while; at her side Rainy wasn't fidgeting at all, I saw, but instead nodded each time the old man paused. I realized that Auntie Girlie was praying, too, and Rainy followed without knowing the words. I tried to do the same but could hear only sounds and syllables, and not the prayer at all.

The prayer continued; Mr. Dionne's words seemed to come faster and faster. The dancers flexed their feet and legs; Crystal raised her chin and smiled at a word, *migwech*, that I had heard the old man say earlier in the prayer. Listening for that word to repeat, I recognized others, *akii, ogichidaag, kiiwedin, Anishinaabeg*. Concentrating, I fell into the rhythm of old Mr. Dionne's prayer, the pattern of words and meaning in the language of the grandparents and of grandparents' grandparents rising and falling, foreign and familiar, *akii, ogichidaag, kiiwedin, Anishinaabeg*.

Finally, a pause and, again, *migwech*.

Behind me, Uncle Noel thumped his cane on the floor. *Hoh*, he responded quietly.

Grand Entry continued with the Veterans' Dance, led by the four flag bearers, who were followed by veterans, who danced solemnly, pausing occasionally to shake a hand offered from the spectators. Junior, I saw, shook many hands, and when he paused in front of Howard the two men embraced; Junior then patted Howard's shoulder and joined the rest of the veterans who danced toe-heel toe-heel, those *ogichidaag* defenders of the land and people.

BERYL DULEBOHN

Dolly and Rose arrived right before the sobriety honoring, still in their cleaning clothes and hoping they would get there in time to see Vernon Junior recognized; they made it just in time to find a chair with the LaForces. Dolly watched with pride as the announcer invited people to dance behind their sobriety warriors after the first circle around the drum. The entire room rose to their feet as the song began; the oldest warrior, Mr. Dionne, entered the circle, dancing in place. Other warriors entered, singly or in small groups, men and women, who approached to shake Mr. Dionne's hand and then step behind him, also dancing in place. When all were gathered, Mr. Dionne took the first step forward and led the group in a low and deliberate step. At the end of the first circle the announcer said again, "Please dance behind your honored one, if you wish."

Margie handed her shawl to Azure, and Crystal unpinned her blue satin shawl from her shoulders and handed it to Rainy.

"Here, you wear them like this." I showed them how to fold the shawls in half, draping them over their shoulders with the fringe down in back and at the sides, and how to grab the fabric halfway up each side with their hands so that the shawls would hang neatly and evenly. I could see that this meant a lot to them by Rainy's happy, crooked smile and Azure's face so still and wide-eyed, taking in all that she could.

"We look like Indians," Rainy whispered to Azure.

"Ready?" asked Sis.

"We don't know how to dance," worried Azure.

"Follow me; do what I do," answered Crystal, and with her fists on her hips led the sisters in a slow single-step into the powwow circle, where they danced behind Junior.

"Give me a hand, Dolly, would you?" said Girlie. Dolly grasped Girlie's left hand in hers and wrapped her strong right arm around Girlie's thin waist; the *mindimoye* rose. She leaned against Dolly but stood upright, her left arm over Dolly's shoulder and her right holding a tobacco pouch high in honor of the dancers.

AZURE SKY

It was sometime after the feast that Margie noticed Crystal was missing.

At some point, during the time that the kitchen ladies were boxing up leftovers and the teenage boys and girls were washing and drying dishes, and the younger men from the halfway house were wiping down tables and chairs and setting up the packages of leftovers for the taking on the big table next to the kitchen, it became clear she had disappeared. Rainy and I had been inspecting clean silverware and serving spoons for any specks or smears and then sorting them into their proper drawers in the kitchen when Margie rushed into the kitchen and whispered urgently with the head cook, who shook his head *Nooo* sympathetically.

"Has anybody seen Crystal?" Margie asked the room. "Was she eating with you, Rainy?"

"She said she was going to change before we ate," Rain answered. "So she didn't get food on her outfit."

"She didn't come back?"

"We didn't see her," said a girl who was wiping down the cupboards with a damp dishrag. "We were about the last ones to eat, and by the time we got our food we were in a rush to clear up."

"Well, tell me right away if you see her," Margie said and took Rainy along to the bathroom, where she told Rain to watch up and down the hallway while she went inside to look. "Azure, you go back to the chairs, will you, in case she comes back there?"

Uncle Noel asked if there wasn't a suitcase missing—hadn't Crystal stashed her blue powwow suitcase in back of his chair? Well, it wasn't there anymore. He told me to find Margie and tell her.

With Rainy keeping an eye out in the hallway, Margie opened the bathroom door and asked, "Has anybody seen Crystal?" The girls washing their hands at the sinks and neatening their hair in mirrors said they hadn't; one helpfully bent to look under the doors for Crystal's moccasins or her new-looking slip-on tennies.

"I bet she ran," whispered one girl to her friend, who looked out the window next to the sinks.

"Are you looking for your daughter?" asked the church lady volunteer at the registration table. "A girl went out the door about twenty minutes ago, in a hurry. She said she had to meet her dad."

"What was she wearing?"

"Jeans, and a blue satin Mesabi Rangers jacket. She was with a boy."

Margie used the telephone in the kitchen to call the police, who called back in less than twenty minutes to let her know that they had picked Crystal up on Mesaba Avenue where she was walking with Duane Blanchard on the narrow boulevard wearing her shiny satin high school jacket and carrying a small blue suitcase, and had been easy to spot. Had Margie known that she was on her way to Minneapolis to see her dad, the officer asked? Did Margie know the boy who was with her? Duane said he was along because he thought it was too dangerous for Crystal to be hitchhiking by herself.

Rainy and I followed Beryl to the church doors where Margie, joined by the powwow announcer, waited for Crystal, Duane, and the police. Ten minutes later a squad car pulled up.

"Are you Mrs. Gallette?" the officer asked Margie. "We've got your daughter here." Crystal and Duane emerged from the back seat of the squad car, Duane half-smiling apologetically and Crystal expressionless, the small blue suitcase held against her chest.

Margie thanked the officer and awkwardly placed her arms around the stiff shoulders of an unresponsive Crystal.

"I'm Ray Blanchard, Duane's uncle," the announcer said. Duane looked at Crystal, who was glaring mightily at him, and then at his frowning uncle and hung his head. "I'll make sure he gets home."

Except for the dirty look she shot at Duane, Crystal ignored everyone until after the squad car drove away, then she spoke.

"Next time," she said.

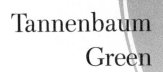

Tannenbaum
Green

AZURE SKY

In the first week and a half after we moved to Dolly and Junior's house, our life as foster girls changed so much and for the better: we didn't even look the same. We had new clothes, beauty school hairdos, and had been introduced to new people, some of them relatives—although it wasn't clear yet how they were related to us, or to each other, some living in Duluth and some at Mozhay. We even had a sort of third- and fourth-hand connection to our mother, which in the mystery of half-spoken phrases and looks between our new relatives, fed our spirits while starving us further. At night we slept in our pink-and-purple bedroom, fixed up just for us, Rain usually holding my hand before she dropped off to sleep. If we woke during the night, we could hear the comforting whisper of Dolly snoring across the hall and the louder buzz of Junior from the pantry/den/sewing room and could see our way to the bathroom, lit by the small shell-shaped light next to the sink. Rain didn't wet the bed once. And on the eleventh day of our new lives we had to start at our new school, Washington Junior High.

At Mrs. Kukonen's we had finished our last year of elementary school and the first two years of junior high together; because Rain had been held back a year after third grade, we were in the same grade and usually in the same classes. Once Rain had learned that school went more smoothly when she didn't cause any trouble (after the situation with Miss Fisketti who lied about the remainder), she stayed quiet, whether she understood what was going on or not. I helped; some of my help required doing Rain's work myself, and most of the time the teachers looked the other way. They didn't want any trouble either.

Why was school so hard for Rain? Although she was so slow that she rarely finished homework or tests, she was passed to the next grade every year. I could have told the teachers that she liked stories but that her attention wandered as she read; that she liked numbers but disliked the trickeries and betrayals of algebra—which we both still passed, me by the skin of my teeth and she by our cheating together on homework and the final exam; that she loved geography and music; that she hated art class and gym. All these things were ignored as long as she kept quiet and didn't cause any trouble.

Actually, we would rather have not gone to school at all, but we did enjoy the shopping trip to Kmart on the Sunday afternoon the day before school started that year. Dolly didn't enjoy the trip especially; she was tired and jumpy. Junior had one of his Vietnam dreams the night before, one that woke him up. His mother had heard the slap-slap-slap of his solitaire game on the kitchen table and got up to make cocoa; then both of them stayed awake playing double solitaire until the sun rose. We left Junior sleeping on the couch with the radio set to the classical station. Dolly said Kmart would be packed for sure—not a place for a guy who needed some peace.

She finished her cigarette with deep, irritable puffs outside Kmart. "This place is a nut house!" she said. "Just look at the checkout lines!"

I braced myself, hoping that she wouldn't grab us each by a shoulder and push us in front of her, like Mrs. Kukonen did when church was crowded.

"Man, oh, man; why did I wait?" Dolly asked. "It's my own fault . . . Oh, well, let's grab a cart. Hey, look how much fun those little kids are having!" We were learning that Dolly always tried to be a good sport.

Dolly and Junior both brought us to school on the first day, when Rain and I would be new ninth graders at Washington Junior— Dolly feeding Junior cues as he drove and parked, and as they walked with us up the stairs into the building. According to Dolly, Junior had had the time of his life at Washington: he had played the trombone in the band, and the concerts were in the auditorium, which was so fancy, and the band went on that trip to Hibbing that time, and he was a good swimmer, and the gym was huge, and he was on the basketball team, and he had a lot of fun with his friends . . .

Junior didn't say much beyond nodding and smiling about the band and gym class, but when Dolly got to the part about his friends, he said, "We had a blast in shop class, Howard and me— remember Howard, from the powwow? Me and Howard, and this kid named Russell, we sure got in some trouble! There weren't any girls there; they took sewing class, I guess." He began laughing. "Good thing! That Russell, remember, Ma, when you had to come to the school?"

"They call it life skills now," said Dolly, "and boys and girls take it together—they do a little sewing, cooking, and a little shop, too. Maybe you'll make those dustpans, like Junior did."

"It came apart, but she still uses it." Before we went into the office Junior gave me and Rain each a pack of gum. "Don't chew it in class," he said, "but it never hurts to have gum on you."

The office had our schedules ready, with all of our classes together, as Dolly had requested, and our lunch tickets. The secretary called to a girl waiting on a bench, who she introduced as Allison, an office cadet.

"Allison is in the ninth grade, too; she will walk you to all of your classes today and show you where your locker is, and the lunch-room." Allison rose, a lanky-haired girl with heavy glasses who looked older than a teacher.

"So now you know somebody," said Dolly brightly. "Junior will be there after school to pick you up; wait at the Fourth Street doors." And they were gone.

"Are you ready?" asked Allison. "Let's go to your locker first, and then the washroom, and then I'll show you to your first class. I will come to your classes when you're done, too, and bring you to the next one."

Allison was a fast walker with long legs and a long stride; as she led us to our classes we skipped a little to keep up and also, as she took her duties seriously, to hear the useful things she had to tell us: "Lots of the girls like to bring things in to decorate the inside of their lockers; let the drinking fountain run a little before you drink because the water tastes rusty; you have Mr. Conkler for civics class—smile at him when you walk into class or he will ask you why so sad, and stay far enough away that he can't rub your back; don't let your bare feet touch the floor in the locker room; the school nurse looks crabby but she is really nice; never leave your locker unlocked; and see that girl over there? Her name is Collette, stay away from her, and don't use the stall second to the end on the left in the girls' second-floor washroom. And I'm assigned to you at lunch for all year: you can eat at our table as long as you want to, but if you decide to eat with other people, you can."

At the end of the day our keeper escorted us to the front door and waited with us until we got into Junior's car.

The next day we were on our own. Remembering Allison's words of wisdom, we brought a picture of a teddy bear cut from one of Dolly's old magazines, which we taped to the inside door of our locker; we showed our teeth to Mr. Conkler and he brushed my back, near my bra strap, with his creepy, overly friendly hand;

like the other girls we stood on the tops of our shoes as we changed clothes for gym in the locker room; I half-smiled at the school nurse, who stood outside her door between classes looking crabby but half-smiled back, nodding her head choppily; we ate lunch with Allison and her friends, all serious, no-nonsense girls who didn't shriek and toss food like the kids who were cutting loose and having fun in the lunchroom.

On the way to English class after lunch I told Rain that I'd be right there and stopped at the girls' washroom on the second floor, which was empty except for two tough-looking girls standing at the mirror who glanced at me and then back at their reflections, one running a makeup brush of blush back and forth across her cheeks and the other fluffing the front of her teased-up black bangs with a brush. I rushed into the second stall from the end on the left and heard one of the girls at the mirror whisper to the other, who whispered back. I heard the *pshhhht* of hairspray, then the rummaging sound of brushes being stashed into book bags. The washroom door opened, and I heard footsteps that became stomps as someone approached the door to the second stall from the end, where I sat perched on the edge of the toilet behind the latched door, and kicked it, twice.

"Who's using my toilet?"

I jumped from my perch, yanking up my jeans.

"Who's in there?"

I flushed the toilet and took my book bag from the hook on the back of the door and held it to my chest for protection as I unlatched the door and opened it.

"Who do you think you are using my toilet?" She was as terrifying in person as I had imagined from my seat on the toilet, and she was big, bigger than me, and angry, angrier even than Mrs. Kukonen had been before Rain said "Praise the Lord our Savior!" and Mrs. Kukonen split the side of Rain's lip. She took a step forward, trapping me in the toilet stall, and I hadn't known I had it in me, but I dropped my book bag on the grimy, water-spattered bathroom floor and got ready to grab her by the shirt, knock her off balance, and then run for my life.

"What's it to you, Collette?" The teased-hair girl had come over from the mirror. Her stance was wider than mine, and she held a can of hairspray in her fist like a weapon.

"She's a new girl; leave her alone." The brilliantly blushed girl was standing next to the teased-hair girl and looked ready to pull back for a punch.

I stepped around Collette and stood next to the two rescuers, thinking the three of us could take her if we had to.

"Well, she better not do it again." Collette went into her toilet stall and latched the door.

"Hey, new girl, we're gonna be late to class," said hairspray. "We're in English with Miss Tallakson, too—we'll go in with you."

"Where's your warden?" This from the girl with the blushed cheeks. "Allison. How do you like her lunch table?"

"Do you know Nolie Dulebohn? We saw you sitting with his grandma at the powwow. Are you related?" asked hairspray.

"We're not related, I don't think—I don't know for sure," I answered.

Hairspray looked disappointed.

"Who was that girl from Mozhay he was talking to? Is he her boyfriend?" asked rosy cheeks, obviously hoping that he was not.

"The fancy dancer in the blue dress? That's Crystal, and he's not her boyfriend."

"I didn't think so," said rosy cheeks happily. "Hey, this is Kim, and I'm Amy."

"Azure. My sister Rain is in ninth grade, too."

We hitched our book bags onto our shoulders and swaggered out of the bathroom. Just outside the door to English class, Amy said, "Ready for Kissy-Face Tallakson?"

Kim snorted; she and Amy tossed their heads, flipping their hair

to the side. I did the same, and then we three bad girlfriends saun-
tered into the classroom.

"Azure Gallette, Kimberly Olson, and Amy Pierre, you are late.
Green slips."

Rain looked horrified. She raised her hand, which the teacher
ignored.

What did green slips mean?

"One for each of you. Let's go, ladies." Miss Tallakson was scrib-
bling on a tablet.

With Kim and Amy I walked to the teacher's desk, where she
handed each of us a small piece of paper on which she had written
our names, circled and with a capital *T* larger than the circle firmly
printed over both. Green slips.

"Bring those to the office; they're going in your files. Not a good
start to the school year, on the second day of class," she said.

Our transgression was awarded by five minutes of freedom walking to the office, handing our tardy slips to the secretary, and walking back to class. Along the way Kim and Amy asked me if Rain and
I would like to eat at their lunch table.

"Since you know Nolie Dulebohn, maybe he would eat with us
sometime, too," said Amy.

We lived less than two miles from Washington Junior, which meant
that we weren't eligible to take the school bus. Dolly said that thinking about us walking by some of the neighborhoods between school
and our house, especially those stretches of vacant lots and woods
above the Point of Rocks, made her nervous and so Junior drove us
to school most mornings before he went to bed. Junior would sleep
until three o'clock or so and then drive back to Washington to pick

us up after school. On the afternoons that Dolly had a cleaning job and needed the car, we walked to the hospital coffee shop in downtown Duluth, which wasn't far from school, just five blocks east and a half-block down the avenue. Dolly's friend Florence Sweet worked there, and we sat at a table by the window and watched for Junior's car. When Dolly got done with her job, she went home and while Junior picked us up she would put her feet up for a few minutes before getting supper on the table.

We loved coffee shop days. Florence watched us from the cash register as we drank our glasses of water (no ice for me; I had a habit of chewing ice cubes loudly, which Florence thought might drive the people who were at the hospital to visit their sick relatives crazy—because it did her) and did our homework, and sometimes someone from the neighborhood would stop by for coffee and pie and visit with Florence, who seemed to know what was going on with everybody in town. Occasionally one of the neighbors offered to buy a pop for me and Rain; we were instructed by Dolly to always say, no thank you, that we had drunk a lot of water and weren't thirsty. That was so that people wouldn't get tired of us, Dolly explained to me. And besides, we shouldn't be filling up on pop. That didn't keep us from accepting an occasional quarter, or even a dollar, from somebody who wanted to give us something.

One afternoon in October we turned down the avenue to the coffee shop entrance and I could see Florence through the window—she had left the cash register and was sitting at the counter next to the old man who read the *Herald* every afternoon, so close that their heads nearly touched. With her forefinger, she followed the words in the news story. Florence and the old man read the story aloud but not in unison, commenting and asking one another questions. Rain and I got our glasses of water and sat next to Florence, sipping as we listened.

"I heard it on the news last night, on WDIO, before I went to bed," said Florence. "Dennis Anderson said that she could be Native American."

"Rolled in a blanket and left in the ditch on Rice Lake Road," said the old man. "It says here that she has long dark hair and is somewhere between eighteen and thirty-five. Who do you think she is?"

"She could be anybody—somebody who comes in here, or one of those young women who hangs out in front of the Twins Bar, or even a high school girl. What a terrible thought." Florence glanced at Rainy and me. "See Junior out there yet? Why don't you girls go look out the window so you don't miss him. Don't go outside until you do, though." She always made us wait inside the coffee shop for Junior to pick us up, and not out on the sidewalk.

"How long had she been there, did they say? Probably not all that long, but still, on the way to the dump things drop out of people's cars, out of the trunk or the back of the pickup if they don't secure the load. Driving on Rice Lake Road I bet most wouldn't even notice until they got to the dump if a mattress, say, had rolled off the pile of junk in the bed of a truck . . . . happens so much that driving by, a person would go right past that stuff; not many would bother stopping to look at an old mattress or a cruddy rolled-up rug. So who knows how long she could have been there?"

"Blanket, it says here. Rolled up in a blanket and dumped there, at the side of the road."

"Somebody will miss her. Somebody from Duluth, or somebody from Fond du Lac or up north who doesn't even know yet that their daughter is missing. They'll pick up the paper and see this, and they'll wonder if it could be their girl. Or maybe somebody will just tell them. Terrible thing, just terrible."

"It was a stranger," Rainy whispered. Florence's head snapped in our direction. "A stranger must have grabbed her." Dolly had told us about strangers, and cars, and vacant lots, bushes, and ditches.

"Are you keeping an eye out for Junior? Why don't you girls go stand over by the window; don't make him wait." Florence was trying to get our attention off the conversation. We obediently picked up our school bags and moved to the windows, turned our faces towards the glass and the street, and our ears to the conversation, until Junior double-parked and we ran out to get into the car.

"I hope it wasn't Crystal," Rainy said just before we opened the car door.

I shivered.

At Dolly's the conversation was about the body, too. Junior had read the *Herald* before he went to bed that morning and had not slept well. Now, sitting at the kitchen table where Dolly served him his plate of hash and green beans, he reread the story. "The poor little girl," he said. "I wonder who she is."

"These young women, they don't know how much trouble they can get into, how much danger is in the world. They could be gone before anybody knows they're missing. Rolled in a blanket and just left at the side of the road. Somebody is going to know who she is. Her poor family."

The story was on WDIO news, but there was nothing more than had been in the morning *Herald* story.

"Well, that will get the word out more," said Junior, "although there have probably been people calling the police already once they saw the paper or heard about it."

"There's probably people calling the police right now—somebody who didn't see the paper or hear about it—wanting to ask about their missing girls," said Dolly. "Whoever she is, God bless her family; they will have a sad, hard night."

But by the next morning, nobody had come forward to say that their daughter had run away, that their sister hadn't come home from visiting grandma, or that their coworker hadn't shown up for her shift. I got up early, before Junior got home from work, read the *Herald* as soon as the paperboy threw it onto the porch, and turned on the TV at 6:54 to watch the five-minute local news. The investigators now thought that the woman was likely older than eighteen, perhaps thirty to thirty-five. Anyone with any information at all should call the Duluth police department.

After school, Nolie and Duane offered to walk us to the coffee shop; Kim and Amy, who lived just east of Washington but on the hillside, joined us. As we walked towards the hospital the dead woman on Rice Lake Road was not mentioned; instead, Rainy, Kim, and Amy chattered about gym class. It had been rope-climbing day, and one girl had gotten halfway up towards the ceiling when she froze and had to be talked down by the teacher. I could not get my mind away from the body and didn't have much to say; neither did Duane and Nolie, who eyed every stranger on foot and car that passed us on Fourth Street.

"She had rope burns on the insides of her legs," said Rain.

Amy and Kim burst into giggles.

"They were all red and scraped up where she was holding onto the rope really tight with her thighs," Rain continued.

Amy and Kim laughed louder and held onto each other, unable to stand alone.

"The teacher sent her to the nurse to get some cream put on them," Rain continued.

"Holy," commented Duane. Kim punched him in the arm.

"Why so quiet, Azh?" asked Nolie.

"Oh, I don't know; too much homework—don't you get sick of English class? So boring; Miss Tallakson never stops talking about herself."

"I just don't listen to Kissy-Face. Try it, it helps pass the time."

At Third Avenue East, Duane and Nolie offered to split up, and one of them stay on their usual route with Kim and Amy and the other with me and Rain (Kim glanced at Nolie and then me, a signal that I should choose Duane).

"Nah, that's all right; it's still light out; we'll be fine," I said, regretting my words as they crossed Fourth Street and Rain and I were left alone: the short walk in those few blocks towards the hospital was uneasy, our steps longer and faster than usual. That afternoon the narrow walkways between houses, stores, and apartment buildings

were not interesting spaces to look into backyards but places of unknown danger, where the light of the sun never reached, where
inside lights were turned on during the day, and shades were pulled
against the eyes of neighbors, whose windows looked directly into
their lives from just five feet away. A stranger, dark-clothed and
evil, might lurk between the basement windows that were covered
with newspaper that tore and disintegrated as it aged, leaving gaps
where an old woman hand-washing her laundry in a stationary tub,
lonely and nosy, might glance out to see two girls, Rainy and Azure,
grabbed and pulled into the basement through the door that she
had forgotten to lock, the stranger knocking the old woman against
the stationary tub so that she fell, her head cracking like an egg
on the cement floor, then dragging both girls into the windowless
furnace room. These were my thoughts, felt by Rainy, who held
tight to my school bag handle with both hands as we walked. My
gait off due to her weight, I stumbled over an uneven crack in the
pavement; she clutched at my elbow. I would have told her to let
go but her grasping fingers reminded me that we were still alive and
that life was precious.

At the coffee shop Rain and I sat at the counter, near the cash
register, in order to hear as much as we could from both the kitchen
and the dining room. Neighbors and regulars stopped by, reading
the newspaper and asking one another if there was anything more
on the news. The murder of the unknown young woman was all
anyone talked about. If she was one of the Indian women from Duluth or Fond du Lac, or one of the reservations up north, wouldn't
somebody identify her pretty soon? Could she be from Canada, or
the Dakotas, a young woman come to Duluth looking for a job and
then, desperate, duped into prostitution?

Prostitution?

Florence asked us if we had homework; we took our history
books from our bags and opened them on the counter, leaning over
them as we listened. I chewed on my hair for studious effect.

The older people talked among themselves about other women who had died tragically, or mysteriously, or disappeared. Charlotte Sweet, who put on her coat and walked down that same Rice Lake Road a half-century ago and was never seen or heard from again. Charlotte's daughter Violet, who in her early teens and not long after her mother's disappearance left town with the Sweets' neighbors, Mr. and Mrs. Bjornborg, her relatives not finding out until she was gone. Julia Ricebird's friend from the dormitory at the Harrod School, who didn't return to school one September and whose father said she had never gotten off the train at Lengby that June. Young women who took the bus to Minneapolis to work in the defense plants or the mills during the Second World War and never came home. Women who left bars with strangers, women whose husbands and boyfriends said they left the house after a fight; women out walking at night in search of earning money in ways the older people at the coffee shop didn't go into. And then, as my head turned toward the windows to see if Junior's car had pulled up, I thought I heard her name whispered. Loretta. Rainy heard it, too.

"Loretta . . . West End . . ."

". . . Amber Flow . . . if that was her, they thought she caught a ride . . ."

"Could have been on her way to Sweetgrass . . . Miskwaa River . . ."

"*Sssshh.*" This from Florence, who puffed her lower lip out delicately in our direction, her frown deepening the worry crease between her eyebrows. The conversations regrouped into pairs and threes and continued, with voices now lowered to whispers; two women at the condiment stand stood closely together, shoulders nearly touching and their bodies in the shape of a V. One touched the other's arm as they carefully kept their eyes off and their attention on Loretta's girls. Me and Rain.

Rain and I turned the pages of our history books, seemingly fascinated by our studies; a hospital security guard paid for a cup of coffee and a roll at the cash register, his badge catching the light from the fixture above Florence's head. He dropped his change into the nearly empty common tin cup, dimes chiming against nickels.

Suddenly, I knew what to do.

I slid off the stool and walked to the windows and waved big, pretending to see something. "Junior just went by! He's at the end of the block, stopped at the lights; guess there was too much traffic for him to stop out front," I said to Florence. "Come on, Rainy; we have to hurry before the light changes."

"What?" Rain, who always listened best when she was doing something besides looking like she was paying attention, raised her face from her book. "Were they talking about Loretta?" she whispered. "Is it time to go already?" she said loudly enough for Florence to hear and, closing her book, she rose and followed me.

"You girls be careful out there; don't jump into traffic and get run over," Florence instructed. "He's early today, isn't he?"

"It's because we have so much homework. See you!"

"Bye, sweethearts; see youse."

It looked like a clear shot to the corner and across the street, out of Florence's line of sight; almost running, we would have made the green light if Rain hadn't stopped short in front of the man sitting on the sidewalk outside the hospital, one leg stretched forward and the other folded up to his chest, with his chin resting on that knee and his eyes closed.

"Howard," Rain said, and because she said his name, even though Dolly and Junior had told Howard that he was not supposed to talk to us when he had been drinking, we had to stop.

He tilted his head slowly, chin still on his knee, eyes rolling upwards towards us and drifting, focusing, drifting. Recognizing. Using the brick wall for support he courteously rose to his feet.

"Boozhoo. You going to the coffee shop?" Howard was not allowed in the coffee shop when he was not sober. "I was just thinking of going there myself, later on."

"No, we're on our way downtown; we've got to do an errand for Dolly."

Bracing one hand on the wall Howard swayed slightly, thinking. He knew that Dolly kept close track of us. "Where's Junior?"

"Oh, he's going to pick us up after."

"Here? At the coffee shop?"

Out of the corner of my eye I saw the coffee shop door open and the security guard shade his eyes; turning his back to the sun he pulled a pack of cigarettes and a book of matches from his pants pocket, turned, and cupped his hands to his mouth.

The stoplight changed to green. "Yes—see you when we get back." I grabbed Rain's sleeve and we crossed the street. I hoped that Howard would forget, or that the security guard would notice his unsightliness and tell him to move on somewhere else, maybe to the sidewalk in front of the Union Gospel Mission.

"What does Dolly want us to do?" Our pace made Rain a little breathy.

"You'll see . . . let's hurry, Rain, okay? We need to get back to the coffee shop before Junior does."

"Let's try to make all the green lights!"

The police department was on First Street, several blocks west of the hospital and three blocks downhill to the left, next to the County building where we had last seen Loretta, that day she gave us to the County, when Rain was four and I was almost three. A block from the civic center I got a side ache but grasped my belly just below the ribs and hitched, keeping up with Rainy though limping slightly. We took the shortcut past where the squad cars were parked at the back and arrived at City Hall, not far from the doors to the County courthouse.

"Do you remember this place?" I asked Rainy. "Do you remember those glass doors, and the ride in the cab that smelled like Christmas trees?"

Rainy stopped, as she always did when she thought. "I remember the man who carried me to the car. Azh, do you remember the northern lights, and our mother dancing to the music that was coming from the sky, from the silver clouds?"

She was remembering the story I had told her so many times, embellished a little from time to time with my heart's wishes, a story that to her had become like her own memory; however, there had not been music in the story up until that moment. "No, there wasn't any music, just the lights in the middle of the night."

"But I remember the music, don't you? It came from the sky, and it sounded like Junior does sometimes; you know, when he sings to himself but there aren't any words?"

"She was dancing with the northern lights," I answered. "But I remember now, there was a rumbling in the wind way far up, and she had wrapped one of the blankets around her because she was cold. Music; it was music, like singing. That's why she was dancing."

I pictured Loretta wrapped in a blanket and left in the ditch that ran alongside Rice Lake Road. "Rain, I have to go in and talk to the police."

"About the murder?"

"Well, sort of."

Rainy's muddy green eyes changed their shape from almonds to large marbles. "Do you know who did it?"

"No, I don't."

"But you have a clue, right?"

"Rainy, do you wonder if that lady could be our mother?"

My big little sister gasped and silently folded her cool fingers into mine. As my hand warmed hers, I felt our heartbeats and strides synchronize—our hurried, urgent walk becoming *Azure-Rain, AzureRain, AzureRain, AzureRain* that last block to the police station.

We talked first to the policeman at a counter, who told us to sit on the bench next to the door and wait right there. We watched him, listening as he punched several lighted buttons on his phone,

one after another, talking in a low voice to three or four people on the other end. We couldn't hear much, just ". . . two girls, early teens, I guess . . . that's what they're saying . . . detective . . . is she out? Yeah . . . not sure, looks like it . . . the chief? You bet."

"You can come inside," the policeman said, unlatching the half-door next to the counter. "You're going to talk to Chief Miletich."

He had the face of an eagle and a neat, straight-backed walk. "I'm Eli Miletich, the chief of police. Come in my office, girls; sit down." He indicated two wooden chairs pulled up to a desk; I noticed that he stood until we sat, then took his own chair on the other side of the desk. He rested his arms on the desk and folded his hands. "What can I do for you? What are your names?"

"I'm Azure Gallette, and this is my sister, Rainfall Gallette."

"Do you go to school?"

"Washington, we're both in the ninth grade. We live with Dolly Gallette, and with our cousin Vernon Gallette Junior, he's her son."

"Oh, yes, I know the Gallettes; Junior used to box when he was a kid. I've seen him and his friend, too, Howard Dulebohn, right? Good kids. What can we do for you today?"

I took a breath. "Well, it's about that story on the news, about that woman; you know, the woman they found, by the road?"

"What about her?"

"We think we have a clue," Rain answered and bit at her thumbnail. I wondered if we looked silly to the chief of police, like ridiculous girls carried away by big imaginations, making up a story that would waste his time just to get attention.

"About who she is." Suddenly, unexpectedly, I was afraid that I might begin to cry. "We know about somebody who is missing."

"Why don't you tell me about it?" He looked straight into me and waited. His eagle eyes softened, like Junior's.

I cleared my throat. "The Gallettes, Dolly and Vernon, they're our foster home. We've been living with them since we moved here from Mesabi—we're Gallettes, too; we're related. We've been in foster homes since we were little, and we haven't seen our mother since then."

"What is your mother's name?"

"It's Loretta Gallette. Mrs. Kukonen said that she gave us away and she doesn't have any rights. We heard people, friends of the Gallettes, talking about how she is missing, but we don't know for how long it's been."

"She has been reported to the police as missing?" asked Chief Miletich.

"We don't know. The lady they found, in the news they said she could be Native American." My voice cracked.

"The woman they found is not Loretta Gallette. We know who she is; we aren't announcing that yet but I can tell you she is not Loretta Gallette."

Reaching for words but unable to find any, I wondered if that cold block of ice I felt at the center of my heart, that stunning chill, was relief.

"Are they sure?" asked Rain. "Azh, are they sure?"

The chief of police pushed back his chair and stood. "I am going to go check something out. Are you two all right sitting here for a few minutes while I do that?"

"We won't touch anything." This from Rain.

"If the phone rings, don't answer it. Somebody else will pick it up at the desk."

We waited silently for a few minutes, then Rain said, "Do you think they're really sure?"

How could I tell my sister that Loretta must be dead, that if she was not the woman wrapped in the quilt and left at the side of Rice Lake Road, she must be some other woman left for dead somewhere; otherwise, we would not have to look for her, she would have found us, whether she'd signed us over to the County or not. Rain turned her head away from me and rested it on her arms that were folded on the chief of police's desk; her shoulders shook, she raised her head and wiped her nose on her sleeve, and bent to untie and retie her shoes. I realized that I had been speaking my thoughts out loud.

The police chief returned; this time he sat back in his chair, his hands on the curved arms.

"There is no police record in Minnesota for Loretta Gallette since 1976, and as far as we can find right now, there is no record of her death."

"So, she's just lost?"

"She was reported as missing in 1979; I cannot give you the name of the person who reported her."

"So, do you think she's just lost?"

"Look, I know Dolly and Vernon, and they are good people. They wanted you to live with them, and they wanted to take care of you. It's not necessarily easy to track down children who are wards, and not easy to get them back. They cared enough about you to do that, and they will take care of you. They want you to have nice lives; they want to give you that, and they want you to grow up to make good adult lives for yourselves. Are you understanding this?"

I nodded and took the slow, slow breaths that I had learned when I was little—inaudible inhalations and exhalations that flattened any waves of pain into a surface smooth as glass, lit by a hangnail moon. Rainy untied her left shoe, loosened it, retied it. "They're not the same tight," she said.

"And I'm not going to forget about this—I will keep you girls and your mother in mind, and anything we find out, we will let Dolly and Vernon and you girls know about it. Right away. All right?"

Sickened, I replied yes and thanked him; Rain double-knotted her left shoelace and rose, expressionless; she forced a smiled as the chief looked into her face and gently shook her hand. He asked if we had a ride home; when I told him that we would walk back to the hospital coffee shop to be picked up by Junior, he told us we would get a ride back in a squad car.

"You take care, Azure and Rainfall," he said. "Connie here will walk you out to the squad—Connie, radio 202 and tell him you're on your way back there, will you?"

"Azure?" Rain whispered as Connie held the door open for us. "I can't remember what she looks like."

"She looks like her picture, the one Dolly showed us."

"But when she was a grownup, when she was our mother? I can't remember."

I tried, and all I could remember was her blanket-covered back against the backdrop of the night sky.

"Have you ever ridden in a police car before?" Connie asked as we walked toward squad 202, but Rain said, "Hey, there's Howard!" and there he was, loitering on the avenue, and a policeman was talking to him, asking him what he was doing, and then Junior drove up with Dolly in the passenger seat in the car. Howard, who had followed us unseen from the coffee shop to the police department, had called Junior from the pay phone in City Hall and then waited outside, watching for us from the corner of the building where he could see both exits.

"Thank God!" Dolly jumped out of the car and put her arms around Rain, then me. "Thank God—oh, don't do anything like that again! What were you doing with the police? Never mind, we'll talk about that later—Howard, thank you for watching over them!"

"It's an honor," Howard answered. He and Junior shook hands, clasping palms up, fingers folded and wrapped around thumbs, the AIM warrior handshake. Dolly offered him a ride back to the coffee shop and asked if she could buy him a hamburger, but Howard knew the rule about how things had to be when he was drinking. He picked up his duffel bag and raised one hand, palm out, towards Dolly, Rain, and me and walked down the avenue, turning in at the alley and into the blacktop and concrete wilds of the city, our warrior guardian angel, our *anjeni.*

. . .

That evening Dolly, with the television on and the volume set low for background, told us a little, just a little, about Loretta—about the surrender of children, about the County, and about ICWA and how we came to live with her. She told us that Junior's father had been lost, too, in World War II.

"So you have that in common with Junior: his dad is lost and so is Loretta. But see, Loretta had a tough time ever since she was born—her parents weren't married and the County ended up taking her away when she was a baby, and then her mother and dad got her back but they couldn't take care of her, so she was raised in foster homes all the way through. She was going to live with Artense's family, your auntie Artense, when they were little girls, and that didn't work; then after a while she was adopted out, but the family returned her when the wife got pregnant with her own baby. She got sent back to the foster system, and she lived all over the place. Then when she turned eighteen she was on her own. Most of the time nobody knew where she was until after she surrendered the girls, and then the County let Mozhay know about it, but Loretta was just gone, somewhere. Nobody knew where."

Dolly told us that some Indians have had hard lives, that there were a lot of broken hearts around Loretta.

"But there's always hope. Junior has hope; he looked for you, didn't he? And after a while he found you."

When we went to bed, cozy and sad under the pink-and-purple quilt that Dolly had picked out just for us, Rain asked me to tell the story again about our mother dancing in the northern lights. That night I continued the story, making up a new part, about how Loretta would show up again one day, like magic.

Sometime during the night I awoke and got out of bed to check on the world outside the window. Pushing the shade aside to look at the night sky, I saw only darkness, no northern lights, no outline of a woman wrapped in a blanket, dancing. If Loretta had been there, if she had turned to look at us, Azure at the window and Rain snoring lightly under the pink-and-purple quilt, I might have been able to remember her face. But she was gone.

The next morning we heard on the radio that the body had been identified; the woman was from out of state, not Native, and we didn't recognize her name.

"Her poor, poor family," Dolly commented. "At least they can bring her home."

Later, I would come to think of that afternoon at the station, and then listening to the news on the radio the next morning, as the point in our lives where we understood we had to just go on, move on. Dolly, perhaps because of the experience she had with loss, made it look easy. Junior and I did our best to follow her lead and succeeded a little more every day, and we assumed that Rain was right along with us. But Rain was not with us; she wasn't moving on. At first we didn't even notice, just as at first nobody had noticed when Loretta vanished. We finished breakfast and got a ride to school from Junior, who then went home and handed the car keys to Dolly, who left for work. Junior washed up, put on his pajamas, and went to bed. After school Rain ran a dust mop over the floors while I shook out the rugs, our jobs for the day, and then put away our clean laundry, folded by Dolly and left on our beds. For supper we went to McDonald's. We understood Dolly and Junior's unspoken words, that supper at McDonald's was a treat to acknowledge the hard realities of the previous day.

As Rain and I finished our cheeseburgers, Junior cleared his throat and told us that from now on we always had to let them know where we were. "You hear that, both of you?"

"We will," I answered. "We didn't tell you because we didn't want you to worry."

Dolly held both our hands as she said, "Azure Sky and Rainfall Dawn, you mean the world to us. We don't know what we would do if anything happened to you."

Junior cleared his throat again and asked if we would like ice cream cones for dessert.

We ate our soft-serve McDonald's cones in the car. Back at Dolly and Junior's, back home, we did our homework, played slap-jack, stayed up to say good-bye to Junior when he left for work, and then went to bed.

For the longest time I replayed the afternoon at the police station in my mind, viewing it like a movie watched by Dolly, Vernon, and me, and then finally Howard, who waved at us with one arm as we drove away, that arm in his ragged jacket sleeve a tattered angel wing—each of us watching the movie with different eyes and spirits. I watched for each of us and squirreled away something that added to my Loretta collection each time I rewound the reel and played it again. Unable to bear watching through Rainy's eyes, I never played her reel—which put a distance between us, not our first and, of course, inevitable in the course of things.

Somewhere in that movie, seen through Rainy's eyes, was a point—some instant or minute or hour during that late afternoon and the next morning—that Rainy finally lost her certainty that she would see our mother again, her belief that all that she had forgotten about Loretta's face would be recalled someday, each feature of young Loretta's worried face transformed into joy and peace by the reunion. I think Rain ceased to continue an integral part of her own existence that day—although outwardly, like me, she grew older every day, watched over by Dolly and Junior and anyone else who had grieved Loretta's disappearance. And over time, as Loretta's disappearance was ultimately accepted as loss, the guilt that existed over not realizing her absence sooner shifted shape into a love and care showered onto her daughters, Azure Sky and Rainfall Dawn.

My bitterness rises unexpectedly sometimes when I think of love that exists because of guilt. But it settles when I remind myself that Dolly shared her backbone of steel with us, the daughters of Junior's true love, determined that in turn we would do the same — strengthened by a good, solid breakfast of oatmeal with sliced bananas. It settles when I remember that Junior rescued us out of love and a sense of what was right and perhaps, yes, a little guilt.

We didn't question Dolly's waking us at 6:30 as she did every weekday; we knew that it was important to her and Junior that we did all right in school and that we graduated. After school Dolly would ask us the question she asked a couple of times a week: "How was school today?" Our answer to the question, which was the same before the body was found on Rice Lake Road as it would be afterwards, was that school was fine — whether or not it actually was. Her next question was always, "Do you have homework?" If we did, we sat at the dining room table and worked at it while Junior watched TV in the front room; if we didn't we could do whatever we wanted, but she always wanted us to stay around the house.

It was harder with Junior. His couple-of-times-a-week question was, "What did you learn in school today?" We always tried to put together something that sounded interesting, something that wouldn't disappoint him, seeing as he took such pride in having brought us back to the family, such pleasure in our living not with strangers but at home, in Dolly's dressing us in clothes we liked, and bringing us to the beauty school twice a year for haircuts and stylings. So we told Junior about what we had for lunch, and about the Anne Frank movie that we watched for history class. Junior would take us to basketball games in the evening before he had to go to work and we talked with girls we knew from school—the whole time Junior not saying much at all, as was his way, but smiling as he watched the game and listened to our chatter, some of it contrived out of consideration for what we thought he would like to hear.

The truth, however, was that my sister hated school.

I helped Rain, where I could, with her homework and in the classes we had together. When we were caught cheating on a true-or-false test in civics class and sent to the office, the counselor at school talked with us both for a long time and then called Dolly at home and made a referral for a special education assessment for Rain. Listening by the closed kitchen door to Dolly and Junior talking about it, I thought it seemed odd, as if the counselor—and Dolly and Junior, too—hoped that Rain wouldn't do well on the test, which was the opposite of what they had always told us to do: study hard and do our best. They didn't say anything like that to Rain this time; nevertheless she worried, nibbling on her thumbnail and biting at her lower lip until Dolly gave us the job of rearranging the furniture in our room, which required dusting, vacuuming, window washing, and making decisions about the placement of the bed and bookshelf, and the order and arrangement of books. Like Dolly, Rain seemed to always feel better while doing these tasks and looked at every little change when it was done and then looked again, perhaps moving a piece of furniture closer to a window or moving the Barbie doll, still occasionally played with, from the dresser to the bookshelf.

Dolly prepared Rain for her assessment by acting as though something really great was going to happen. "It will be a test just for you. There will be a lady who comes to give it to you at school; she's really nice."

"Do you know her?"

"Well, no . . . but Mrs. Berg says she's really nice." Something in the way Dolly said that made me think of how she told us that getting a shot at the clinic wouldn't hurt.

"You don't have to study for it." This from Junior. "And they want you to bring a snack."

Rain stopped peeling her thumbnail cuticle. "Can I bring chocolate-covered raisins?"

"Sure."

Sis covered for Dolly at their afternoon job at the Elks' Club so that Dolly could go with Junior to the meeting at school about Rain's assessment tests. The news, a disappointment yet not a disappointment, was that Rain had not tested into special education. The counselor and the assessor said that Rain's assessment did not indicate learning, emotional, or behavioral disabilities, and that while there was the possibility of "undiagnosed" learning challenges, she would remain in regular classes.

"So nothing happens?" Junior asked.

"She doesn't qualify for special services."

And that was that. We finished ninth grade and left Washington.

We settled further into our home with Dolly and Junior and enjoyed the summer before high school. Sis took over more of the cleaning jobs in order for Dolly to spend time with us: we watched a lot of TV, rearranged the furniture five or six times, and started learning to sew. Occasionally we took the bus to the mall with Kim and Amy; passing the bus stop in front of Central High School, we craned our necks for a glimpse of the freed, adult tenth-graders we would soon be, Rain silent as we chattered.

Once we began high school Kim, Amy, and I found that we were not nearly as free and adult as we had imagined, but we did as Dolly said we would: we got used to it. Rain, rattled by the change, didn't adjust to high school and never did graduate. Her attention drifted during the classes she attended, which were few, yet she mysteriously passed half of them—probably because her teachers couldn't figure out what to do with her. Sometimes, instead of going to class, she followed me to mine and spent entire afternoons sitting in the hallways, waiting for me. When she grew tired of sitting on the floor, Rain occasionally rose to half-heartedly sway and dip toward the reflections cast by the overhead lights onto the patterns and cracks of the tiled walls and floors. But only when she was alone. As she became more fearful and began to not recognize people she should—which again we didn't notice for the longest time—Rain would huddle up against the wall and wait for rescue: me at the end of the bell. She was sitting outside of English class—where I was listening to the smartest and dullest girl in class read her most excellent and excruciatingly dull paper out loud to the rest of us, the great and captive unwashed—on the afternoon that Nolie was taken off school grounds by the police. Rain, watching through the window next to our shared locker, saw the whole thing.

Kim went to "pregnant school," which was what we called the quarters in the school basement where the classes for girls who were pregnant or new mothers were held—special classes that included women's health (and, no doubt, contraception instruction). From everything Kim told us it was a pretty nice setting and schedule—and for the new mothers it was a real relief from the realities of taking care of an infant: classes were shorter, and in between they got to see their babies. Rain would have loved a schedule like that, and helping out with the babies—but that part of the school was off-limits to everyone except for the teen moms, their babies, and their teachers. This included Kim's boyfriend, Nolie Dulebohn who, incarcerated in the Arrowhead Juvenile Center, had taken off one day during outdoor recreation time to hitchhike to Central to see his and Kim's baby, Little Lucas. Nolie was standing at the basement window, bending down to wave at Lucas, who Kim was helping to wave back, when the assistant principal, on his afternoon walk around the school scoping out smokers and skippers, asked Nolie what he was doing. Nolie ran down into the woods in back of school and through backyards and alleys to Kim's mother's house, where a police car was waiting. He held his hands high in the air and kept them there while he was patted down by the officer, who let him ride uncuffed in the back of the squad car back to the AJC. His time was extended, but with good behavior he would be out in time for Kim's graduation.

"Freddie-Boy Simon's coming down to see graduation, too," Amy told me with a significant look and a snicker, which I ignored.

Early in the spring of the year that I was a senior and Rainy a junior, Dolly had talked with me privately about going further in school in the fall, to the Vo-Tech or even UMD. Junior would like that, she said—he had wanted to go to college himself. He had enlisted in the Army instead and after his four years were up had thought about using the G.I. bill to go to UMD; he had even gone up there to look around and brought home an application. Part of the way through filling it out he told Dolly that he didn't think he was smart enough to go to college, and he put the application in his dresser drawer.

"Do it for Junior," Dolly said. "It would mean a lot to him."

I was accepted at UMD and was signed up for freshman orientation in late June. I had worried about Rain's feeling left out and so had put off telling her, but Dolly told me not to worry; she had asked Rain if she would like to go to work with her and Rose for a while, take a break from school. She let Rain tell me herself that she had found a job and would be earning some money.

"If we have too much work, you can help sometimes, too, for pay," Rain told me, echoing what must have been her own private conversation with Dolly, "but college will have to come first."

The school gave every graduating senior four tickets to the ceremony; I invited Dolly, Junior, Rain, and Sis.

Dolly thought we should have a party on a Sunday afternoon near the end of June. Sis offered to bring a fruit salad, and Junior to paint the front door. The paint was peeling so that he would have to scrape down to the wood and prime it, he said. Would we like it painted white again, or a color? Rain and I could decide, he said, in honor of our being done with school. We both thought a deep green would look good with the gray siding and roof.

At the paint store we picked out a shade called Tannebaum Green that the four of us agreed would be perfect all year round, and especially at Christmas. Junior offered to paint the door frame a nice Green Bay Packers gold, so that everyone would know which NFL team he liked best, but Dolly declined. Behind her back he scowled and pouted, which made Rain laugh; when Dolly turned around to see what he was doing, the expression on his face became angelically innocent. He did this three or four more times while the machine mixed the paint, rumbling and shaking, lurching then slowing and finally stopping, and then he was finally caught. Dolly rolled her eyes, and we were all giggling as the clerk dropped mixing sticks and four flimsy white painter caps into a bag. At the cash register Junior took one of the caps from the bag and put it on his head sideways, again frowning ferociously but this time also sticking his tongue out sideways at Dolly, who was counting out bills to the cashier. Dolly glanced at Junior and did a double-take; Rain and I started giggling again.

"That's a beautiful family you have here," the cashier remarked to Dolly. "Your granddaughters sure have a great time with their dad."

I realized then that whether the cashier had our relationships right or not, we were in fact a beautiful family. It is my favorite memory of us.

We cleaned the house and made everything sparkle, even the glass in the picture frames, lovingly wiping the faces of Junior and his father, Winnie, Ingrum, Maggie, and the last few years' school pictures of me and Rain, which Dolly had placed in the center, having rearranged everyone else to surround us in a big circle. She bought a new shower curtain and steam-ironed her lace tablecloth on low, spreading it over the dining room table while it was still warm and damp so that it would dry in gracefully draped scallops.

At the party store we bought graduation paper plates, cups, and napkins, all matching. Sis borrowed the smaller coffee urn from the Legion, the one used at weddings and showers.

And then Junior died, on a beautiful Monday morning the day before graduation ceremonies in early June. After an ordinary night at work he clocked out, rinsed and dried his thermos, set it in the bottom of his wiped-clean lunch pail, and said hello to the first-shift security guard as he went out the door. Standing on the sidewalk, waiting for a truck to pass before he crossed the street he paused, turned his head to the left, to the right, and then to the sky; he raised one arm as if waving at the pickup. The driver slowed and returned the wave, and Junior slowly collapsed, first to his knees and then to his right side, dropping the lunch pail and lying on that side, pillowing his head on his extended arm. Within half a minute he was no longer breathing.

Junior's funeral, a mass, was held four days later, three days after the graduation ceremonies we didn't attend. Rain and I sat with Dolly in the front row of St. Mary Star of the Sea, along with Sis and Florence; Howard, who sat on the other side of Florence, rose just before the mortician closed the lid of the coffin and placed an eagle feather in Vernon's folded hands, which also held a small crucifix. Back in the pew he reached across Florence and Sis to hold Rain's and my hands for a few seconds; Howard's hands were, like his eyes, warm. In back of us were Vernon's friends from work and AA, and relatives from Mozhay half-filled the church and the social hall downstairs where the church ladies served ham, potato salad, and cookies.

And just like that, with Junior's death, things went to pot, as Sis would have said. Things happened so quickly in the first four days after he died that we had no time to grieve until after the funeral was over and everyone went home, including us. Even then, grief had to wait: the first thing Dolly did that evening was go over the bills, the checking account, and her and Junior's joint savings account, which was nearly empty from the funeral expenses. Junior had one last paycheck owed by the hospital and a life insurance policy for nearly ten thousand dollars. The relatives at Mozhay had collected almost four hundred dollars cash, which Margie had given to Dolly before going back to Sweetgrass. There had been more than five hundred dollars enclosed in sympathy cards that the funeral home guarded carefully and gave to us in a white card box that said *Remembrance* on the lid; inside were also the guest book from the funeral mass and, discreetly at the bottom, the itemized funeral bill. Dolly made out a check to Dougherty's and wrote "Paid in full" across the bill, which she kept in the box with the sympathy cards.

Sis came over the next day to talk about the daywork business, which she thought they could try to expand some, if that would help. Dolly thanked her but said it wouldn't be enough to keep us in the house, which still had a mortgage.

"I'll look for a job," said Dolly. "Maybe Rain could clean with you, instead of me."

"Where are you thinking of looking?" asked Sis. She didn't say aloud what she and Dolly were both thinking: that Dolly was over sixty and hadn't worked at a regular-paying job in years.

Just then there was a mournful bark, followed by a high-pitched retching sound, from under the kitchen table. Jennifer, old and nearly blind, had vomited up her food and was lying on her side, panting. Dolly picked up her frail Yorkie and cradled her gently.

"I've been getting myself ready for Jennifer to pass; I knew it would be hard," Dolly said. "But Junior—how can this be?" The four of us wept, carefully stroking and patting Jennifer's patchy, lusterless sides.

Golden
Manor

AZURE SKY

As it turned out, college was out of the question because I needed to work. In a way, I felt relieved that my destiny for the foreseeable future was set and I slept peacefully the night that Dolly and I came to the decision. Who would I have gone to college with anyway? Kim had started at the Academy of Hair Design right after graduation, and Duane enlisted in the Air Force. Kim, expecting another baby in November, was hoping to marry Nolie. Whenever I ran into her, she talked about getting their own place; in the meantime, she was living with her grandparents and working part-time at a day care. Rainy, excited about earning money and helping out at home, had her own feelings of relief at being done with high school. In the midst of the shock of losing Junior and the dull grief that followed, I felt oddly set free, as though one of his parting gifts to me had been a pair of wings.

Dolly, however, fretted, especially after Sis told her that she didn't think Rainy's replacing her in their daywork business would work for the long haul. Rainy was too scatterbrained for daywork, Sis said bluntly: she had to be watched all the time, was so slow and not fussy enough. If their regulars, the East End ladies and the

Legion, didn't like the job they were doing, they would find somebody else to clean.

"Dolly, my girl, you know that Rain is a good girl, but it takes a lot of time to keep an eye on her when we're on the job. She is going to have to do something else besides daywork, you know that. The Legion already asked last time I was there with her if we really needed to send two people out there, and I had to show them how Rainy was hardly getting paid anything once you look at the billing, but they still looked at me funny. She can't help it but she moons around so much when we're at people's houses, and you know how it has never been that easy to keep the jobs going." Dolly should stay with the daywork, Sis thought, and Rainy could do something else, her and Azure both. Azure was smart enough—she could work in a store or in an office maybe. As for Rainy, well, if Azure got a good enough job, Rainy could stay home and take care of the house.

Dolly took another drag on her cigarette. "I'll quit these things; that will save us some money." She snuffed the end gently and thriftily, saving it for later, in the souvenir ashtray Junior had brought home from Okinawa.

"You do that, and when Rain is home by herself, you, me, and Azure can call her up just to check on things. Florence said she would call, too; we can all take turns."

Dolly looked doubtful.

"And, look," Sis continued, "Rainy can go along to help sometimes, once in a while, like to the Bishop's house after his Christmas party."

It was Florence from the coffee shop who found the job at the Golden Manor nursing home laundry for the both of us, Rainy and me. Florence was friendly with the Golden Manor cook, who told her one day that the man who'd done the laundry for years had gotten on at the County nursing home, where he would get insurance and retirement benefits. The cook told Mr. Nilsson, who owned Golden Manor, that he could get two young, energetic girls for the cost of one man, and that she and Florence could personally speak for our honesty and reliability.

By August, Dolly had turned Junior's room back into a sewing room and pantry, I had my driver's license, and Rain and I were settling into our job at the Golden Manor laundry room in the basement next to the caretaker's tiny apartment, which must have been as hot, steamy, and bleach-scented as the rest of the basement. Our job was to collect, wash, sort, and deliver laundry for all the residents at the Golden Manor Convalescent Haven. We did this every day except for Sundays and Wednesdays—Rainy on bed linens and towels and me on everything else, because she didn't have the patience for sorting, especially clothing. Rain did, however, enjoy rolling the clothing cart through the halls and delivering sweat suits and pajamas. And we took pride in bringing home paychecks, in helping Dolly keep up with the house payment and bills. Except for having to get up at 5:00 to start work at 7:00, we enjoyed the work at Golden Manor, for a lot of different reasons.

Golden Manor is full of stories massed and crowded, the memories and words of the residents elbowing each other for space. For someone with my habit of reading everything I see and listening to everything I hear, those stories glide, limp, soar, and crawl in forms that do not consist of letters and written words, or sounds and spoken words. There were hidden stories made visible in the marks and symbols of food, blood, and waste that I, the senior laundry worker at Golden Manor, read as I pretreated each one (start with a soak of cold water, soda, and salt for blood and body waste; go right to a hot-water soak for grease from food and gravy) and load them into washing machines at the proper water temperatures (hot for kitchen and bath towels, sheets and pillowcases; medium or cool for clothing, always separated by whites, colors, or darks). When each load was completed, I looked for them again—the stories erased or so faded that they could no longer be read, that fading and erasure the Golden Manor standard of cleanliness. Anything readable went back for the soak-and-stain treatment. It was not until they were out of the dryer (highest temperature for the kitchen and bath towels, sheets and pillowcases; medium for most colors and darks; low or line dry for brassieres, stockings, and other delicates) that I checked for thin spots or fabric tears and decided what would be thrown out, torn into cleaning rags, or mended with a back-and-forth zigzag stitch on the sewing machine kept open on one of the work tables in the laundry room.

In that place of fading memories, the residents in their shared double rooms above my head on the main floor struggled to keep legible the stories of their lives, stories that for all I know eventually existed only in the soil marks in their dirtied laundry—cryptics that were erased with presoaking, detergents, and bleach. How could their stories continue, then, except with the marks of each day's living: of cereal and cocoa spilled on the lapels of a bathrobe; of vegetable soup on a pink sweatshirt embroidered on one collar's wing with a kitten; of a half-chewed gravy-soaked piece of Swiss steak bounced from a set of dentures to a sleeve, then a pajama leg, and onto a washable terry-cloth slipper? Of a tearful begging for help from a harried nurse's aide for a trip to the bathroom, or a change of soiled bedding?

Those stains and stories replenished and reinvented themselves in the canvas carts that Rain and I wheeled from the main floor hallways to the elevator and down to the underground world of the senior and junior laundry worker and the old man who was the caretaker of Golden Manor. In honor of the residents I read what I could—a sleepless night when frightened Mrs. Jorgenson thought only about her son, Myron, who was hit by a car and killed while hitchhiking from home into downtown early one morning on his way to his job at a bakery. Myron's specialty, the Parker House rolls, didn't appear on the shelves that day; in her bed at Golden Manor, she fretted about that, worried that he would be fired, then remembered that he had died. On bad nights Mrs. Jorgenson scratched her arms in her sleep, short pink stripes of blood that dried brown on the sheets.

At Golden Manor, Rain stopped dancing when alone as she had when I was in class at Central. Frightened of some of the residents, Rain often delayed the delivery of clean laundry to their rooms by dawdling as she folded bedding, matching and rematching top to bottom, corner to corner, her eyes so close to the fabric she couldn't help but see the ghosts of stains that could never be completely removed—and that distressed her as much as some of the residents frightened her. The trouble with Rain was that although she couldn't read the stories, she felt their sadness in the faint shadows of their imperfectly washed clothing and bedding; in the soaking and scrubbing of their soiled laundry she felt their losses and grew melancholy and more fearful.

The afternoon before Rain was let go from Golden Manor we took the bus to the beach at Park Point and waded up to waist-deep in Lake Superior, which rarely warms but keeps an icy feel to it even on the hottest days of summer. Chilled, we abandoned the water for the sand and lay down side by side on the sun-heated and itchy wool camping blanket that Junior had given us in high school, a Pendleton and nearly new. Within two minutes Rain was snoring in her slow-paced, dreamless way, and I was both chasing and resisting sleep in my sleep-avoiding way, succumbing as always at some never-remembered point to dreams from which I always wake unsettled.

Lying on the camping blanket next to my sister, older but who seemed younger every day, I felt the muscles in my back begin to relax and surrender to the sun-warmed sand that had formed to my body in much the same way as the heating pad placed beneath Mrs. Maki at Golden Manor in the hours before she died. My eyes were closed against the glare of the sun, just as Mrs. Maki's had been against the glare of fluorescent lighting. But my eyes were not closed to the dreams: I replayed the day of her death, the sweetly natural passing of an aged mother out of her grown children's lives, and on to the cloud in heaven where she would sit for eternity, playing her harp. That is what she'd told me once while I was covering the end of her bed and her waxy, yellow feet with an extra flannel blanket I had run through the dryer to heat.

"Oh, my, that feels good on my cold tootsies," she'd said. Beneath the flannel blanket her feet relaxed, drooped. Perhaps they were melting from the heat.

On the day that Mrs. Maki died I had delivered a clean cover for the heating pad and collected the soiled one. I had tapped on Mrs. Maki's door: "Linens," I said to identify myself. "Good afternoon, Mrs. Maki," I continued, glancing at her closed, wrinkled eyelids. "I've brought a nice, fresh cover for your heating pad."

Mrs. Maki's son, who had been sitting next to her bed watching the news, left the room while the nurse's aide rolled his mother to her side and I changed the cover. When I left, holding the bundle of sheets and soiled pad cover, he whispered, "I don't know how anybody does this job," and handed me a dollar.

"Thank you, but we can't take tips," I said, handing the dollar back. He tucked it into the pocket of my Golden Manor smock.

The day before Rainy was laid off at Golden Manor was also the day we saw Freddie Simon in his swimming suit at the Park Point beach, a long bus ride from home. As I lay next to Rainy on top of the camping blanket that scratched at the back of my thighs, I closed my eyes, avoiding a dream by thinking about Mrs. Maki's wrinkled eyelids, and if she might have been faking sleep when I changed the heating pad cover. She also might have been avoiding dreams, or perhaps just the overhead fluorescent light, or the aide, who I knew she disliked, because she confided in me that she hated being around heavy people. Had she been listening to the news, I wondered, as the lulling warmth of the heating pad had sent Mrs. Maki to sleep? Lulled, I slowly sank into the heating pad . . . and jerked, awake. Was it the heating pad or was it the sand? I asked myself in near panic, wondering where I was and who I was, my clenched eyelids lit by the two o'clock sun to translucent hot blood oranges, shutting out most of what I didn't want to think about on my day off:

the laundry room at Golden Manor

the shift supervisor, Mrs. Rooney

the light bill, due two days before payday

Instead, because I could feel the cool dryness of her body temperature, lower than my own, I thought about Rainy, lying next to me on Junior's Pendleton camping blanket, her arm brushing mine as had become our habit in sleep. I suspected Rainy actually liked working in the laundry, but she would make five o'clock the next morning as miserable as she could for both of us because she hated getting up early. I was almost always tired these days.

And then, as I was pulled into sleep, all of that was on the other side, and Mrs. Maki rose from her bed, telling me to take a little rest, that she would take care of the laundry this afternoon, and so in my dream I was lying on Mrs. Maki's heating pad that was really the warm sand of the Park Point shoreline beach. Back of my eyelids, tiny white seeds drifted across the orange-red of the darkest fruit into random patterns of curling grape tendrils that pulsed, broke, rejoined. Broke, rejoined, and pulsed. Pulsed, lulled.

A sigh rose unexpectedly from far, far back of my ribs and was interrupted by a gasp and long inhalation; in sleep I left Mrs. Maki's bed and Golden Manor and took the bus downtown to the library, where I wandered through the stacks alone and silent past shelf after shelf of books, my fingers trailing along the spines of romances, travel books, mysteries, a cookbook. Which stories might choose me, I wondered? As I reached to touch the plastic cover of *Villages of France*, I realized that I had forgotten my overdue books at Sherry's house and had no way to get back to Mesabi to retrieve them. With a sick feeling, I realized that I had lost my borrowing privileges at all of the libraries in the world.

But not to the discards—those broken-down books too old, stained, worn, or read to near death that had been rejected and removed to the limbo just inside the library's front doors, a row of battered open cardboard boxes and an uneven revolving rack that squealed when it was turned. On my way out I picked an exhausted-looking paperback with fanned, yellowing pages from the rack, a paperback that had been opened and closed so many times that the spine was a concave row of cracked vertical white stripes. The front cover was a blur of letters green, blue, and purple, glowing illegibly across a winter night sky, the blur running down into the impressionistic dream picture on the cover, which in turn sharpened in focus to become the fire escape outside the back door of the apartment where Rain and I had lived with our mother when we were little. The night of the memory, the night she had taken us out the kitchen door onto the fire escape to see the northern lights dancing in the sky.

"Waawaate," Loretta had said. "Waawaate; that's the northern lights." Colors danced in the night sky as she wrapped a blanket around me and Rain, turned to face the lights, swayed, dancing into the waawateg, and left.

I half-woke, bereft and grateful to leave the dream where it was. In the past. Where, of course, it waited for me to fall asleep again—my barriers down, it would return as it always did.

Loretta left us here in the darkness where blood oranges purpled and cooled in shadow at the back of my eyelids. Clouds, I thought. Rain later on. I pictured the heavy raindrops hitting the sidewalk in front of the apartment building later on the day that I had awoken to my mother's whisper—splattering to jagged-edged circles the size of silver dollars, drops on drops on drops. The city scent of steam rising from sun-heated concrete.

A coolness of shadow passed across my face. Rain stirred, turned, and kicked a sprinkling of sand onto my legs; I woke and without opening my eyes realized that the city scent of steam rising from concrete was the dampness that comes in the absence of sunlight. Shaded, the breakdown of microscopic life below the top layer of sand renewed itself in a dank pungency that was unsettling to think about: births, ingestions, digestions, deaths going on below the plaid camping blanket that absorbed my perspiration on that hot afternoon into its woolly scratchiness.

The shadow passed. Again, hot red-orange light. Again, cool purple shadow. A cloud, I thought, that passed before the sun and stopped. Rain's fingers against my upper arm above the elbow wiggled, drummed, disappeared.

"Hey, where are you from?" A Native man's voice, soft and teasing.

I heard Rainy wake as she muttered and sat halfway up, leaning on one elbow. Grains of sand scattered lighter than snowflakes across my shoulder and jaw. I brushed them away and opened my eyes, touching to check the zipper of my Golden Manor uniform smock I wore over my swimsuit. It had not worked its way down as I slept; the V of my tan line would stay at my collarbone.

He was a large, dark silhouette framed by an eye-dazzling sun. As he lifted one hand in greeting, the heavy-set shadow that covered half of my body and all of my sister's moved wide stripes of light across our swimming suits, Rain's red bandanna-print two-piece and my one-piece tank suit, the ugliest I had ever seen—a rubbery-looking brown cut indecently low in the chest but clearance-priced to a quarter at the St. Vincent de Paul store. I wore a bra under the suit and kept the top covered by my Golden Manor uniform shirt zipped to the base of my throat.

"Good afternoon, ladies." He waved at another man who was

writing something lengthy, upside-down to me and too far away to read, into the sand at the shoreline. "Freddie-Boy!" he called, his open shirt exposing a cluster of puckered burn scars covering his right breast and side. The sand writer stood, waved, walked toward us. His thin legs, untanned and much lighter in color than his thicker upper body, gleamed whitely in the sun.

Rainy stared. "A-azhure," she said in her sideways lisp, "look at the big"—the man's outline tensed, he clutched at his open shirt, which he closed and buttoned—"muscles he has!"

She was of course smiling up at him, and her overbite and the gap between her two front teeth made her look younger than she was and eager to talk to him. Her mouth, raspberry pink against suntanned skin the red-gold of a new penny, dipped ever so slightly on the right side as it had ever since Mrs. Kukonen's fist, crimped into a deceptively knowing-looking crease. Her almond-shaped eyes, this afternoon the green of deer moss, narrowed sleepily and then widened, fixed on the stranger, unblinking.

"Are you Shinnobies?" he asked. "Do we know each other?"

We answered simultaneously.

"We were just leaving," me reaching for my sandals.

"Indians!" Rainy smiling and taking in the shorter man's round face, his sun-browned pot belly, and the paler palm of the hand he offered, which she grasped and pulled as she got to her feet. "We're Indians! What are *you*?"

He laughed. "That's rich. Are you the little sister?"

"No, I'm not the little sister. Azure is."

"Pretty name, Azure; what's yours?"

"Never mind what her name is. Like I said, we were just leaving."

"Rainy. I'm Rainy Dawn."

"And you're sisters?"

"We're half-sisters! Azure's half, and I'm half."

"So, are youse Anishinaabe, is what he meant. Ojibwe?" This from the sand writer, the shorter, more rounded silhouette approaching us. Short-and-Round took off his sunglasses and squinted. "Hey, do we know each other?" He hitched up the back of his swimming suit, which had worked its way to the bottom of his pot belly in front and below the waist in back—and I recognized him: Freddie-Boy, from the sobriety powwow Junior had taken us to when we first got to Dolly's. Pushing and shoving, laughing with some other boys at the drinking fountain: as he had bent to take a drink, another boy had yanked at his sweatpants, pulling them halfway down so that we had seen his underwear. He had yelped, pulled up his sweatpants, and run down the hallway and out the Coppertop's basement doors.

He was taller but still chunky and still recklessly wearing comfy elastic waists, I noticed. I saw that we were about the same height and then—who can explain the mysteries of the universe?—I was at that moment riveted at the sight and presence of the sand writer: his white feet, his translucent hazel eyes; my fingers, left to their own instincts, would have reached to touch his hair, fine and silky looking as a baby's. I would have rested one arm on each side of his strong-looking neck and clasped my hands lightly behind his head, against his black hair, and I would have rested my chin on his shoulder and my head against his ear, and I would have felt his heart beating, and everything would have been all right.

Instead, I took a deep breath to clear my head. "And we're on our way home. Come on, Rain, let's go; we're going to miss the bus."

"Do you remember me, Freddie Simon? From Mozhay?" the sand writer asked. "This here is John Ricebird. Would you girls like to get something to drink at the concessions?"

"We would be pleased to buy you ladies a Coke," said John. He removed his sunglasses, his flint-black triangle-shaped eyes squinting a little in the sun and his full lips puckering slightly as he pointed them towards the snack shack. He looked confident and ready to kiss, which annoyed me.

"No."

"A ride home? We've got a car."

"No. Thank you."

"Walk you to the bus stop?"

"No."

The bus driver ground the gears; the bus belched and jerked forward. Brown fumes hot and oily blew in through the open window.

"Rain, you can't go talking to people we don't know."

"Oh, Azh, they wanted to buy us a Coke. I'm so thirsty."

"They were strangers. Talking to strangers is dangerous. Remember?"

"That one guy, Freddie, he knew us. Do we know him?"

"No, and we don't want to."

"I'm sooooo thirsty. How come you're so mean?"

"Remember about that girl who got her head cut off, that one in the paper that time? Who do you think did that to her? I can tell you who; it was a stranger! Maybe some stranger she saw someplace who just started talking to her. Maybe even at the beach."

What I couldn't say to my sister was what was always with me and with her, too, whether she was aware of the thought or not—that a stranger, someone as harmless-looking as two young Indian guys at the beach, could have offered our mother a ride in a battered, rusting car, that she might have accepted the ride and got into the filthy front seat of a car that had no heat; on the floor was a crumpled McDonald's bag smeared with ketchup that got on her shoe, that as she bent to wipe the ketchup from her shoe the car accelerated; she lurched, and she and the stranger laughed. "Put on your seatbelt," he said.

For Rainy the thought of the beheaded girl was plenty; for a long minute my sister chewed her thumbnail. Then, "A-azh? I think I left my bag at the bus stop."

RAINY

If Azure wasn't being so mean, we wouldn't have gotten thrown off the bus, and it's not my fault the way she has to wear her Golden Manor shirt over her swimming suit so it makes her look like an old lady; that was what made her so crabby in the first place. I explain this to the bus driver, remembering to use exactly the same voice as when I talk to our boss, Mrs. Rooney, at Golden Manor. Slow. I talk slow, and quiet, too, with a deep breath before each thing I need to say.

When the bus driver doesn't answer, I talk a little louder, and a little faster, which of course means my S's start to sputter and get in the way, and I have to try and not spray him, because people hate that.

But to show I know he is in charge of the bus, I call him sir and I remember to hold my hands together behind my back so that I don't touch him.

The whole time he is ignoring me as he talks to Azure, until my hands all by themselves let go of each other and start tapping the metal rim of the bowl we drop our fares into, so that it starts to rattle like it thinks I'm pounding in change—my left fist heavy *chong-chongs* like nickels and my right, lighter *ching-chings* like dimes.

"You're going to have to take her off this bus," he says, to Azure and not to me. "Walk her home, cool her off. How far is it to home?"

He hands her two bus tokens and he won't even look at me. He's mad because he had to stop the bus. I reach to unbutton the top button of my blouse so that he can see how good I look in my red bikini top, because it has its own built-in foam rubber bust pads, but then I remember that at the beach house I changed back into my bra and without the foam rubber bust I hardly have anything there at all. And my swimming suit, the red bikini that is mine and not Azure's, is in the beach bag that I forgot at the beach house, on the wooden bench that is the bus stop. And Azh is jealous about the red bikini that is mine, because I saw it first at the St. Vincent de Paul store, and she had to take the other one, the one she says makes her boobs look gross so she has to wear her Golden Manor shirt over it, and that makes her look like an old lady. That is why Azh is being so mean, I start to explain again.

He's acting like he can't even hear me, and so I talk louder yet and my S's and words go all crazy. "Sssir, listen . . . listen to me! What-ch the matter, are you deaf or what? Maybe you dust jon't hear Indians, is that what it is?"

The two-way radio above the steering wheel spits and crackles. "Bob, everything all right there?" a woman asks.

"Everything's fine, Cindy. No need to call the police but stay on the line a minute; these two young ladies are going to walk home."

The police. My sister's forehead wrinkles like a monkey's, and her mouth purses up like a raisin, and she thinks she's giving me this dirty look and I almost laugh but . . . the police.

I close my mouth, button back up, and smile at Bob like I do at Mrs. Rooney when she walks past the laundry room door at Golden Manor, checking up on us to make sure we're working.

"Everything copacetic now, Miss? You going to get off the bus like a good girl?"

I nod.

". . . *bzzt* . . ." It's Cindy again. ". . . okay, Bob, got it. I'll hold for the all clear."

Azure tells the bus driver again that we're sorry, and thank you for the tokens, and then she holds out her hand for me to take. We walk down the stairs and out the door holding hands, and these guys sitting in the back start to make fun of us, but I don't care because she hardly ever lets me hold her hand anymore.

The guys watch us out the back window as the bus leaves and we can see they're still laughing, so I give them the finger with the hand that is not holding my sister's. Azure tells me to never mind, don't pay any attention to them. We stand there on the sidewalk holding hands, and just when I think she's going to open her mouth and start telling me how hot it is and how we have to walk home, she says, "The hospital is just up the hill. Let's walk over there and see if we can find somebody in the coffee shop who could give us a ride."

We stand there on the sidewalk still holding hands, which are getting sweaty, and just as Azure opens her mouth again, this time for sure to tell me how hot it is and how if there's nobody at the coffee shop we will have to walk home, a rusted-out Pinto slows down, honks, and stops. I recognize the man who gets out and waves. It is the big man in sunglasses from the Curve, the one who said his name was John who might have cut off some girl's head.

"It's that stranger," I whisper and pull Azure's hand. "He followed us!" I pull harder. "Run!"

Doesn't she remember about the danger? She just stands there frowning, shading her eyes with her other hand, the one that is not holding mine.

The stranger bends to reach for something inside the Pinto, and I am so scared that no sound comes out of my mouth when I try to ask Azure if she remembers about that stranger who cut off that girl's head. Did he use an axe or a saw that he kept on the floor of the passenger seat of the murder car? My heart pounds and the scream that I am trying to force through my throat squeaks and then stops as the stranger holds out my beach bag and says, "Little sister, I believe this is yours."

I can't figure out what Azure does next. If that stranger could cut off our heads right there in the middle of the street, why does she walk up to the Pinto and take the bag? Why does she talk to the guy on the passenger side, who gets out to talk with her, and he is shorter than Azh so that he looks up a little when she says anything.

He keeps his mouth closed while he smiles and probably smiled just like that while he helped his friend hide the body. He looks like he is going to start dancing and doing tricks each time that Azure says anything; finally he opens his mouth wide and laughs, and I see that he has a big space between his front teeth, like mine.

Then the strangers want to give us a ride in their murder car to the hospital, but Azure says no but it was awful nice of them to bring us our bag. She even turns around and waves when we walk away.

"Gigawaabimin!" calls the fat guy.

"See you sisters around," says his friend.

My sister takes my hand again; there is nothing I can do but trust her.

AZURE SKY

Nobody knew that Mrs. Jorgenson could get out of bed by herself, much less that she could find and walk down the stairs, but that is what she did, shuffling her way noiselessly in her fuzzy gripper socks down the hall to the basement stairs. It makes me sick to think how one slide, just a half-inch off, would have sent her flying down that poorly lit steepness. Once at the bottom of the stairs, she hid around the corner, where the corridor turned in an *L* to the furnace room, and waited until I had passed, my attention on the load of bedding, then she ghosted silent on her stretchy socks into the laundry room. While I pushed a box of folded sheets up the roller belt that Mr. Nilsson had installed next to the stairway that went to the linen closet on the first floor, Rain was reading laundry labels and folding underwear and gowns that she sorted into neat piles.

Mrs. Jorgenson appeared like an apparition in the doorway of the laundry room where Rain was alone and picked up a ladies' sleeveless pink undershirt.

"Did you wash this by hand?" she asked. "Were you careful with the ribbon?"

Not wanting to lie, Rain smiled nervously.

"My mother picked this out for my trousseau," she said. "Feel it; isn't it soft? Elmer just loves me in it; whenever I put it on it drives him crazy. You can wear it sometime if you want; you look good in pink. Just ask first before you borrow it."

Mrs. Jorgenson was not alone. Behind her, her roommate was watching. Miss Anderson, who had been a teacher and reminded us whenever we saw her that she had eyes and ears in the back of her head and would catch us if we tried to steal anything from her room—also that she had to keep an eye on that cheap floozie Olga Jorgenson—Miss Anderson had heard Mrs. Jorgenson thumping down the hallway and followed her noiselessly down the stairs, hiding from my sight in that sneaky way of hers.

"I knew it!" Miss Anderson exclaimed triumphantly. She grabbed the undershirt from her roommate's hands, rapping her on the knuckles with the imaginary ruler that was the side of her hard, bony teacher hand. "That's *my* pink undershirt with the ribbon on it," she said.

"It is not either, you dried-up old prune! Go find yourself a husband, and if you can't do that, then maybe your mother will buy you one." Mrs. Jorgenson tried to pull the pink undershirt from Miss Anderson, who pulled back, calling her a cheap-looking tramp.

"*Give . . . it . . . back*," Miss Anderson hissed through her teeth, giving the pink undershirt a hard yank that pulled it from Mrs. Jorgenson's hands. Off balance, Mrs. Jorgenson fell, her fleshy behind making a plop sound as it hit the linoleum floor. Miss Anderson declared that she was ready to give that fat hussy a lesson she wouldn't soon forget. Rainy stepped between the two and was hit sharply across her left ear by Miss Anderson's ruler hand.

"Help! Somebody help!" Mrs. Jorgenson called, her wail winding to the top of the stairs, where I let go of the laundry box, which shot back down the belt fast but not as fast as I ran and only slightly faster than Mr. Nilsson, who had just walked past the basement door when Mrs. Jorgenson shouted.

In the laundry room, Rainy was shielding Mrs. Jorgenson from Miss Anderson.

"What is going on here?" asked Mr. Nilsson. "Is she hurt?"

"Give me a hand; help me up—she won't get away with this," said Mrs. Jorgenson grimly.

Miss Anderson, still holding the pink undershirt in one hand, slapped Rainy across the face with her other one.

Rainy burst into tears. "Miss Anderson, you shit, you fucker," she began; her tirade, louder than her explanation about our beach bag to Bob the bus driver, was filled with profanities I had no idea she even knew. I reached to hold my sister's hands; she whipped them away. "We hate you, we all hate you," she said to Miss Anderson, flapping her hands.

In a calm voice Mrs. Jorgenson, who was still sitting on the floor, said, "Myron, your shoe is untied." She gently touched Rain's foot; Rain quieted as the old woman cupped Rain's heel, straightened her sock, and tied her shoe.

"There—that's better, isn't it?" asked Mrs. Jorgenson.

"That boy of mine, he never can keep his shoes tied," she explained to the room.

Mr. Nilsson sent Rainy home in a cab, then called Dolly and told her he really only needed one girl in the laundry and would keep the big one.

"You need to get some help for that other one," he said. "I'll lay her off so she can get some unemployment, but you really need to do something about her."

Five years later, when Rain was twenty-four and I twenty-three, we were doing all right with my full-time job at Golden Manor and Dolly's daywork, when Sis wrenched her knee getting up from scrubbing the stairs at the Legion. It was her own fault, she said; a person with any sense at all would know not to lift a full bucket and try standing up from kneeling at the same time. The Legion paid her clinic bill, just the same, which was nice of them she thought—but after she had recovered as much as she was going to, she decided to quit her cleaning jobs and move to the new elder apartments at Mozhay. Dolly picked up all of her cleaning jobs and took Rain along to help, since Rain really couldn't be left by herself by that point and I was gone to work from 6:30 to 3:30 every day. Mr. Nilsson was really good to us: he gave us a turkey every Thanksgiving and Christmas, and a ham at Easter, and said he felt bad that he could afford health insurance only for me and not for Dolly and Rain, too. Dolly, however, had her Medicare; Rain used the Indian Health Service clinic downtown on Fourth Street; and we just kept our fingers crossed that she wouldn't break anything or need her appendix out—we would have lost the house and gone bankrupt for sure.

One summer weekend after Sis had moved to Mozhay, we took an overnight trip to the LaForce allotment at Sweetgrass. Sis had come down to the Indian Health Service clinic at Fond du Lac to get a tooth pulled ("See, I was born with too many teeth and they push each other around," she explained, "so every once in a while they just take one out") and wanted some company along on her drive back to Mozhay. She thought that a couple of days away from Duluth would do us some good; we would sleep overnight at Auntie Beryl's, next door to the allotment house. Freddie Simon would drive us back on Sunday and then swing over to Fond du Lac, where he was working on a summer road crew.

I thought we might like staying overnight in the cabin at Sweetgrass, but being the original building and smack-dab right in the middle of the reservation, as Dolly put it, it lacked the modern amenities of Beryl's trailer, which had running water, an indoor bathroom with hot and cold running water, and a kitchen with an electric stove and refrigerator. We could visit the cabin, though, to look around at the place that had been in the LaForce family for almost a hundred years.

Although we had been to Mozhay before, to the school for the spring powwow and feast a couple of times with Junior—and once, when Dale Ann Dionne graduated from college, to a lunch party at Beryl's turquoise-and-pink trailer that was a block or so from the allotment house if you took the shortcut through the woods—we had never been in the cabin. We had seen it from the woods, and from the road, but we never had a wish to actually go there: it had looked deserted and, to me, haunted. I told Beryl and Dolly that Rain was scared of the place, and so because we had known Margie and Crystal since the sobriety powwow at the Methodist church, Beryl always invited them, too, to the trailer when we visited. She privately told Dolly that Margie was probably embarrassed for other people to see the place anyway.

Beryl was always up for company on a short visit or overnight. She had a hard time getting used to living alone after Uncle Noel had died. Because the house was too quiet, she kept a stack of extra blankets and pillows on the bed in her spare bedroom hoping, though she never said it aloud, for guests who snored. On those nights, she imagined that Noel was still alive and she slept well.

At the time of this visit the cabin was unoccupied, as it often was: Zho Washington, whose family had originally lived on the Sweetgrass property, had left Margie and Crystal "high and dry" (Sis's words) and they were staying at Beryl's, Margie in the spare bedroom and Crystal on the front couch. Because we were guests, Margie would be giving up her bed to Dolly and sleeping on the couch; Crystal would be giving up the couch and sleeping on the front room floor with Rainy and me.

Zho Washington had moved into the empty LaForce house with his son Michael after he had parted company with Michael's mother, Lucy Dommage. When Margie was pregnant with Crystal and had needed a place to go, Zho took her in, and Margie and Crystal lived with him in the house until the year before our visit, when Lucy became terminally ill and Zho moved to Minneapolis to help care for her. Margie, unable to manage the work of keeping up the LaForce house, which had no plumbing except to the kitchen sink, had moved into Beryl's trailer until Zho came back ("She's just waiting out that Lucy, waiting for her die," is how Sis explained it to Dolly).

We arrived late on a Saturday morning after stopping at the gas station near the RBC tribal office at the Dionne Fork to pick up some jelly doughnuts and dollar buns that had been brought in earlier from the bakery in Mesabi. We ate the buns with the lunch Beryl had prepared, macaroni and cheese dotted with peas. The jelly doughnuts we saved for breakfast.

After lunch we walked with Beryl, Margie, and Crystal over to see the original cabin. It was the house that our great-grandmother Maggie LaForce was born in, Beryl explained, and it had stayed in LaForce family hands since Maggie's father, Half-Dime, had been allotted his forty acres. Crystal had been born in the same house, and Beryl's trailer was on the allotment, too.

"It's a pretty place, isn't it?" Margie asked as we approached our family home. "And look how clean-looking the yard is." She glanced at Crystal, who frowned. Margie laughed silently to herself at her inside joke.

The shingled house was small, with a shallow porch across the entire front and an attached shed on one side that opened onto a good-sized wooden stoop. On the far edge of the yard was a wooden outhouse with a slanting one-piece roof, squeezed within a stand of lilac bushes. In the yard an untidy stack of firewood leaned against a small shed with a padlocked door; a vinyl-covered clothesline hung between the shed and a thick, rough-barked tamarack that swayed slackly in the wind. In front of the house a driveway, narrowed by the sumac determined to take back its homeland, led to a large mailbox nailed to a sawhorse; farther away in the distance was Lost Lake, blue under the bright early-summer sky.

"Can you see — look hard because everything is greening so fast — can you see the sugar maple stand, way past the backyard?" Margie asked.

We looked hard — we did see it. Margie was right, the place was pretty, and more.

"That's where Zho maple-sugars, or Michael sometimes, when Zho isn't here," said Margie. "People have maple-sugared there in the spring for years and years, including your Great-Grandpa Louis and your Great-Grandma Artense, and before them Zho Wash's mother and dad, and his grandma and great-grandma. Just imagine . . ."

I tried.

"Sometimes I feel like I can almost see them."

Ghosts. My stomach writhed just beneath the breastbone; I breathed slowly, deeply and turned to look at the real, living people I was with.

Inside, the little house was tidy but damp and unused-smelling. The kitchen area was at the side of the larger main room and held a cupboard, wood cookstove, a heavy-looking square table, and four mismatched chairs. A ruffled curtain, sun-faded maroon flowers against thick green leaves, drooped slightly from a braided length of twine nailed to each side of the window. The braid rug at the door to the back stoop and shed was streaked with mud from the soles of a carefully wiped pair of men's winter boots; dried leaves stuck to the streaks of mud.

"Those are Michael's old boots—my mom puts them on to walk to the outhouse, it's so muddy," said Crystal. "If you have to go, use the front door and go over to Auntie Beryl's—the outhouse is gross."

"Oh, Crystal, you know it's always nice and clean in there," said Margie.

"Do you have to go?" asked Sis. "Put on the boots and use the outhouse; give Beryl's septic tank a little rest."

Rain shuffled closer to me, nudged me in the side with her elbow. There was no way she was going to use the outhouse.

"Want to see the rest of the house?" asked Crystal. "Here, there's just the bedroom." A bare mattress on a full-size bed, an upended orange crate with a small lamp on top and a stack of Margie's thumbed-through paperback novels underneath, a clothes rack with empty hangers. "She keeps the sheets in the cupboard." Crystal opened a television cabinet; in the space where a television might have been was a stack of sheets and quilts, with two pillows on top. "I was born in the bedroom, can you believe it?" A picture of Margie giving birth on that bare mattress or, worse, on the sheets stacked in the television cabinet snapped into my mind; I quickly shooed it out.

In the kitchen Beryl, Sis, Margie, and Dolly were sitting at the kitchen table, Margie absent-mindedly moving a heavy crocheted trivet from the center of the table and back. At the center of the table was a round, plate-sized stain darker than the rest of the wood.

"We keep an eye on things, didn't get a single critter in the house all winter except for a few mice, but then one of us is here just about every day. It's nice here in summer, but I think Margie and Crystal are better off with me until Zho gets back, whenever that might be." Beryl raised one eyebrow and tipped her head towards us, and their conversation stopped: we were too young to know whatever the real story was.

"The yard looks nice, raked up so neat like that, and the porch all swept and the windows washed, too. Looks like the cottage in the Snow White movie," remarked Dolly. "Really, it's just darling, isn't it, girls?"

Beryl and Margie exchanged looks and half-snickered. "Heigh ho, heigh ho," Beryl sang.

"Oh, Crystal did the whole thing herself," said Margie. "She didn't need any help at all with the yard!" which made Beryl laugh out loud.

"My, that must have been a lot of work," Dolly remarked. "Nobody helped her?"

"How about that nice Freddie Simon, the young one—you know, Fred's son? Did you think to ask him?" This from Beryl. "He's just like his dad, isn't he, always doing nice things for people."

"And I think he might be kind of sweet on Crystal," added Margie.

"Oh, really? A college boy, good to his mother and a hard worker, smart and nice like his dad? Wuh," said Beryl.

"He has a girlfriend, Auntie," said Crystal. She poked me lightly in the side, unseen by Margie and the aunties.

"When he's sweet on you?" asked Beryl.

"You know, that Rhonda Ylatapa, the one who waitresses at Agwaching sometimes? She goes to college over at Bemidji? That's his girlfriend," said Crystal.

Beryl sniffed. "If Crystal asked him to help her around the allotment, he'd be her boyfriend just like that." She snapped her fingers. "No doubt about it. All she'd have to do is ask."

Crystal snorted. "I'm sure he's just dying to."

Crystal was just the kind of girl that Freddie would like, I thought.

"Oh, he'd do it if we asked him, no doubt about it—but Crystal said she didn't need anything from anybody—or what she really said was *we*, that *our* yard was our own business and we didn't need anything from anybody."

"She said that to Freddie?" I asked, my voice a little tight.

"No, not to him . . . it's like this," Margie began. "No, you tell it, Beryl; Crystal can chime in. I'm sure she'll want to." She picked up the package of cookies Beryl had put out for us and passed it to Rainy. "We got the Chips Ahoy just for you girls—here, take more than just one, sweetheart."

Beryl began. "All right, well, about two weeks ago we were at the RBC on our way to the store for groceries, and Theresa, Margie's friend, you know? Well, she's working at the front desk sometimes, and she says to look at the bulletin board, there's this notice up that there's gonna be some VISTA volunteers coming up to Mozhay to clean up around the RBC and in people's yards. I asked her what are VISTA volunteers and she tells me it's like a club."

"It stands for Volunteers in Service to America, and it's these people who travel around doing things at schools and other places," said Margie. "They read to little kids, and shovel snow for old people, is what Theresa said, and they asked the RBC if they could come up here and clean the place up."

"You should have seen them, *Beverly Hills, 90210* all duded up in designer work clothes," said Crystal, "like they're going to send Tori Spelling, all wide-eyed, just waiting for her turn at the two-seater over at the edge of the powwow grounds, looking for the light switch!"

Margie pursed her mouth to let her daughter know that she was getting ahead of the story. "So, anyway, the RBC thought there wouldn't be enough work to do around the building, and so they put up this notice that said these VISTA people would be stopping by people's houses to clean up their yards if they wanted, that we could sign up. So me and Beryl signed us up—Beryl said that she thought the yard could use some shoveling out—the wood chips around the stump where we chop wood were such a soggy mess, and maybe a new coat of pink paint on the mailbox."

"Grace Dionne was at the RBC when we were, she was there for coffee," said Beryl. "You know they have free coffee for elders, and she lives just across the road, and she hates to pay for anything. You know how she is. Well, she said she didn't want anybody snooping around her house, but with Roy so crippled he can hardly move, she was going to sign up. She said that she would put their name on the list and just keep the curtains closed. Not much chance of that, a nosy-pants like Grace; she never wants to miss a thing."

"I heard that once they got there she came out of the house and really put them to work," said Margie. "You know how she is—she had them washing windows and scrubbing the stairs, oh my, and stayed with them every second! So, anyway, we put our names on the list too at the RBC for the VISTA workers to clean up around Beryl's, and it was a pain in the butt to get all ready every morning and wait for them because we didn't know what day they would be coming, and in the meantime we didn't mention it to Crystal, and she was staying at Theresa's all week hanging around to help out with the younger kids because Theresa's at work all day and Michael is in the Cities again—you know his mother is still sick and he's there with Zho . . . Crystal and Merilee stayed out of trouble, I hope, while you were there—"

"Trouble? How much trouble could me and Merilee get into, stuck out there in the bush, watching those wild kids?" asked Crystal. "So, anyway, Michael came back and he dropped me at the allotment driveway."

"Why the allotment driveway? Why not Beryl's driveway?" asked Margie.

Crystal didn't answer the question; instead, she continued the story. "I got dropped off and went up the driveway to the house and went inside, and it was chilly so I went out to get some wood for the stove. Everything was so damp, even the newspaper, so it took me a while to get a fire started, and I was blowing on the kindling trying to get it going, and I almost set fire to my hair, and then—"

"Always tie your hair back when you're starting a fire! How many times do I have to tell you?" This from Margie.

"Anyhow, they were at the wrong place," Crystal continued, "went right by Beryl's and up Zho's driveway, through all those bushes; got their car scratched, I think; then there's this stamping and pounding from the front porch, and I look up and there's these assholes looking in the window!"

"Were they standing backwards then, young woman?" Beryl said primly.

"Auntie!" said Margie; everyone laughed except for Crystal.

"Right there in the window, waving and pointing at the rakes and shovels they are carrying, big stupid smiles, getting so close they were smearing Chapstick on the window."

"Awww, they wanted to help," Margie prodded Crystal. "So then what do you think Crystal did? She goes out on the porch and asks them what they want, and they tell her they're from VISTA, there to clean up the yard, and Crystal says to them—"

"I said, 'You've got a problem with our yard? What's the matter with it? What makes you think you can just show up here like you own the place? This is Indian land, got it?'"

"Nothing like fighting with the VISTA kids who me and Beryl were waiting for, and we had the paint ready and everything!" said Margie.

"Then she shows up," Crystal pointed her chin towards Margie. "My mom comes running through the shortcut in back, and she's barefoot in the mud—"

"A real jack-pine savage, that was me, running out of the woods—no shoes because I heard Crystal, she gets so loud, and I didn't want her chasing them away—and one of the girls goes running back to the car, she thought I was chasing her!"

We shrieked, Dolly holding her stomach and Beryl dabbing her eyes on her sweater sleeve.

"So I explained they were at the wrong house, and they turned the car around and went back down the driveway and came to Beryl's, and they did a nice job, didn't they? And the mailbox looks cute—that one girl got the plastic roses out of the shed and washed them up and wound them back around the post. They look like new."

"We fixed them something to eat after all that," said Beryl. "We had a really nice time, but Crystal, she was all *manaadiz*, too crabby to come over, so while those kids were doing that work and then eating—big appetites they had, the girls' as big as the boys'— she cleaned up the yard at the allotment all by herself."

"Maybe next year I'll sign up to be a VISTA worker. *Not*," said Crystal.

"That reminds me: did you get to the shed?" asked Margie.

"Not yet."

"Well, if you girls are looking for something to do, how about if you straighten things out in there? We're going back to Beryl's, but you all don't have to—Crystal, you want to take the car to Mesabi after supper?"

"Maybe. We'll hang around here for a while; if you guys want to help in the shed, we can do that, or we can go to town."

Beryl seemed to be shrinking, I thought, as I watched her walk with Dolly, Sis, and Margie on the path back to the turquoise trailer. The aunties were showing their age: Sis's step was slower than I remembered, and her feet swollen; she was shorter, and her chest and arms thinner. Beryl looked tired; her hair, teased and sprayed into its black beehive, listed slightly to one side. Before they disappeared into the woods, Dolly took Beryl's arm; at Margie's light touch on her elbow Sis waved her away.

"Crystal is sure full of beans and *boogids* today," Sis remarked.

Margie's mourning dove voice floated back through the woods. "She could do a lot worse than Little Freddie."

"You can keep your fingers crossed," Beryl's fluting robin's song replied.

Dolly rasped unintelligibly, a cigarette-throated crow.

Cackles, then their voices were absorbed into the leafy air. Sis, limping, paused and turned around, giving me a long look.

We walked around to the other side of the house, out of the sightline of the picture window of the trailer, and sat on the damp, splintery back stairs. Crystal took a pack of cigarettes from her sweatshirt pocket and we lit up and smoked. We talked about work, and then the family, and when we paused we looked out into the woods, past the outhouse toward the sugar maple stand. At some point as the conversation continued, Rain stopped listening; instead she watched the woods, her attention on a tree branch waving in the wind, on dried pine needles skittering down the outhouse roof, on the path back of the outhouse towards the sugar bush. The place was haunted, Crystal said offhandedly; it was one more reason to avoid the outhouse. She could almost picture Shigogoons LaForce ordering her husband Half-Dime around in maple sugar season more than a century ago, she said.

"If she's haunting the place, she probably puts Michael's boots on before she goes in there. Auntie Artense was named after her—Shigogoons was the old lady's nickname. If she's anything like Artense, can you just see her covering the toilet seat with newspaper and kind of hovering over it while she pees? Then she clomps across the yard in Michael's boots and sits on the steps right on the spot where we are—spooooooooky!"

I looked but didn't see Artense or Half-Dime; instead, Margie, very young and very pregnant, rose from the step next to where Crystal was sitting right now; she paced over the yard between the back stoop and the outhouse in her great-grandmother's very steps, counting the minutes of her contractions and breathing the sweetgrass-scented air of the allotment on the afternoon before Crystal's birth; beneath her flannel nightgown the breadth of her belly tensed and relaxed, tensed again. Zho Washington opened the back door and called softly, "I am bringing you a cup of tea, Margie-ens."

"They're walking right through each other," Rain said under her breath to herself.

Did she see them? "Hey, Rain," I said uneasily. "What's the

story, Morning Glory?" But she didn't answer. "What do you see out there?" I asked, hoping that she would say it was a bear and we could go inside the cabin and close the door.

Next to me, Crystal took a long drag on her cigarette, then exhaled a long stream of smoke. "I see it, too," she said to Rain.

I stood, ready to run, and was saved by the sound of tires on dirt and gravel at the end of the driveway. "Hey, do you hear a car?" I asked.

"Freddie," answered Crystal. "He's going to take us to Mesabi— he'll have Rhonda with him and her boyfriend."

"Rhonda's not Freddie's girlfriend?"

"Don't tell Margie."

"Does Freddie have a girlfriend?"

"*Gawiin*; he's all yours. I was just messing with Margie; she is so easy to freak out."

"If I had a mother, I would never do that," said Rain.

"You have a mother," I said. "We have a mother."

Ladyslipper
House

AZURE SKY

The Tannenbaum Green on the front door looked good for a long
time. We stored the gallon of leftover paint on a shelf in the dri-
est part of the basement, and the lid was thoroughly and securely
tamped down after we used it to touch up the door, carefully brushing over any thin-looking spots on the wood, generously but without
squandering. Junior had been right: good-quality paint was worth
the price. The rest of the house was something else: Dolly had her
daywork jobs, but she had slowed down noticeably after Junior's
death. When the new elder housing apartments had opened at Mozhay and Sis retired and turned all of her private home jobs over
to Dolly, that brought in some extra money for a while. But even
with Dolly's daywork and me working full time, we seemed to be
always living inches from the edge—after paying the bills there was
nothing left over to keep the house up the way Junior would have.
As Dolly aged she kept right on working, bringing Rain along on
heavier jobs to lift and carry what she could not physically handle.
The private home ladies, noticing this and worried about liability,
canceled their appointments one by one until Dolly and Rain were
down to just the Legion and an occasional diocese job.

Mr. Nilsson eventually decided to contract with a company to take care of the Golden Manor laundry and offered me full-time work as a nursing assistant instead. He paid for the course and put me on the daytime shift, adding seniority hours and pay from my laundry room work, and kept up my single health insurance. Then he hired Rain back for two afternoons a week sorting the residents' clothing—she did that in the staff break room, which was the former laundry room in the basement and was now kept locked at the top of the stairs for the safety of the residents. We nursing assistants delivered the laundry ourselves to the residents in our assigned wings.

Suddenly, though it wasn't really *suddenly* at all, things started falling apart with Dolly's house. The roof began to shed shingles and the blower developed what sounded like a cough when the heat kicked in, both issues beginning around the same time so that we finally had to admit to one another that the plumbing and windows had been rattling a little more noisily every day, the pipes whenever the toilet was flushed and the windows when a heavy truck drove by or the wind gusted. I folded up a flattened cardboard box and wedged it between the toilet pipe and wall in the basement; the rattle was muffled for only a day. We lined the windows with rope putty and caulk, which worked well to absorb the rattle but not the cold that seeped inside during winter months. The clothes dryer died; we strung a rope from the garage to a pine tree in the backyard and hung our laundry outside to dry; we strung another in the basement for days when it rained or snowed.

I cracked a molar in my sleep; the dentist bill set us back on groceries for months, which worried Dolly. "What if something happened to Rain—say, what if she broke a leg? What if we couldn't make the house payment?"

Sis advised us to schedule Rainy for a complete checkup at the Indian Health Services clinic downtown as well as an appointment with an IHS social worker, and she came down from Mozhay herself for the meeting. The social worker recommended an assessment for disability services, and it was Indian Health Services that finally diagnosed my older smaller sister with Fetal Alcohol Syndrome and possible early-onset dementia. The doctor believed that her dementia might be related to her FAS but told Dolly and me that there was no way to determine that with certainty. He asked if there was anything else from her medical history that we could think of. Why tell him about our lives before Vernon and Dolly's as foster children, or our lives before that? we thought. What would have been the point? My sister was failing; she would continue to fail.

Dolly applied for a home improvement loan and then a refinancing of the mortgage; both were denied. Getting ready to leave the house for the Legion one day, she slipped on a scatter rug and sprained her wrist.

And then, miraculously and mysteriously, the Mozhay Point *anjeniwag*, the Mozhay Point angels, raised their wings and flew invisibly over that hundred-mile-wide swath of ceded territory that was, treaty or not, the homeland from Onigamiising to Sweetgrass— from the Dionne Fork to the Miskwaa River—of the Muskrats, La-Forces, and all their extended families by heart, blood, and, finally, birthright. This was instigated by Grace Dionne, whose house at the Dionne Fork across the road from the Mozhay Point RBC building and the Chi Waabik Casino and Resort gave view of and access to important and interesting Mozhay comings and goings.

Grace was famous at Mozhay for her obsessive tidiness and suspicious nature, as well as for an extreme thriftiness that some said bordered on stinginess. Every morning she checked out the front room window to see that the RBC secretary had arrived by 8:00, then gave her a half-hour to get the business day going and coffee perked in the urn in the former staff break room, which had been taken over by Grace and her senior partners in crime and renamed the Elders Lounge. Then Grace took her clean coffee cup from the drain board in the kitchen (she always brought her own cup; there was no reason to trust the janitor to do anything more with the RBC cups than give them a rinse and not wash them at all), locked her front door (she always kept the doors locked, even when she was home), and walked across the road to the RBC, where she would be the first to arrive for coffee. Every other Thursday she brought a small plate of chocolate chip cookies, made by hands that were knobby with arthritis and rough-skinned from years of scrubbing the rectory at the mission church. Grace's cookies, which Noel Dulebohn had nicknamed "tooth-breakers," were dunkers: greasy, overbaked, and hard to chew.

It was the pausing to dunk Grace's cookies, nibble the softened part off, and dunk again that gave the elders some time to ponder what Sis and Beryl had to say one Thursday morning in the Elders Lounge about the situation that Loretta Gallette's girls were in, down in Duluth.

"They're about to go under," explained Sis. "See, they'd have to refinance the house to get it fixed, but with Dolly not working anymore, they're living on what Azure makes; Azure couldn't get credit to buy a house, but even if she could, then their payment would be higher and they'd owe on it for another twenty years. I told Dolly they could just sell the house to somebody with money to fix it up, that she could come up here and stay with me; somebody else at Mozhay would let the girls stay with them, and Azure could get on at Convalescent Care the next time they need to hire an aide."

"Dolly can't live in Elder Housing," Grace pointed out. "She's not a band member, or even Indian. And there's not room in your place, anyway—you'd have to share a bed."

"Grace, we are Anishinaabe here," said Beryl, "and there's always room—who here didn't grow up in a house not much bigger than the rooms at Elder Housing?"

"I didn't." Grace, who was from the South, put on airs once in a while; consensus among the elders was that she had probably been born in a shack somewhere in the Bayou, but she tried to give the impression that she had given up a Scarlett O'Hara lifestyle for Roy Dionne. He must have really been something for Grace to give up the plantation at Tara for him, is what Sis had commented at coffee one morning when Grace was home operating, Bayou-fashion, on Roy's big toe, which had an ingrown nail.

"We are Anishinaabeg, that is so, but Elder Housing rules only allow for band members. Dolly could apply; she was the mother of a band member, but she would probably stay at the bottom of the list. And that wouldn't help with the girls."

"Dolly says she can't die without knowing the girls have a roof over their heads," said Sis.

Earl LaForce looked up from his coffee cup, which he had been peering into waiting for his chocolate chip cookie to dissolve. "What in the Sam Hill does she mean by that?"

"They're not girls anymore; they must be well into their twenties. Old enough to take care of themselves." This from Grace.

"The one can't; you know, the older one."

"She could get into a group home. Dolly sells the house, she moves to an apartment, Azure gets married, everybody has a place to live. Problem solved."

"If they get out of that house, and the way things look they probably should, they ought to move up here. Azure gets a job up here at Convalescent Care and they all move to Mesabi. Dolly sells the house and moves into the senior apartments at Mesabi, and Rainfall goes into a group home in Mesabi."

Beryl set her coffee cup down hard on the table. "How many of you were on the RBC when Junior Gallette was trying to find those girls? How many remember the work that Artense and Shirley and Fred Simon did to get them tracked down? I've said it before and I'll say it again: it was a long, hard road to the Indian Child Welfare Act, and though it's not perfect, it's what we've got. We are still in mourning for the children we lost, and that includes the girls' mother; we lost Loretta and there's no use in blaming and pointing fingers, but we lost her long before she disappeared, and she may never be found. How can we not do what we can to take care of her children?"

"We can start by helping Dolly understand the situation she's in." Grace crossed her arms firmly across her chest.

"She knows the situation; she also knows what she wants."

"That brings us back to where we started. This is a sad, sad situation when we can't even help our own young people." Beryl's hand shook; her cookie dropped to the tablecloth and rolled onto the floor, where it clattered.

"Leave it," said Grace. "I'll bring it home for the dog."

"What did that poor old dog ever do to her?" Earl whispered to Sis.

Boy Dommage retrieved the cookie. "By God, I'll help if nobody else can—I can write them a check right now for a hundred dollars! Who's with me?" He rapped the cookie lightly on the table for emphasis and then handed it to Grace Dionne, who put it into her purse.

Pearl Minogeezhik, who up to that point hadn't said a word, spoke. "Mozhay should buy that house and turn it into a group home. The band would own it, and I can tell you if my son runs it the way he runs his businesses, we'll make money." In partnership with his mother, Jack Minogeezhik, reservation entrepreneur, owned a gas station and convenience store, a construction company, and two apartment buildings, one in Mozhay and one in Duluth. He was also an elected representative to the Mozhay Point Reservation Business Committee. "We can send a proposal to the RBC."

"You mean us? We're gonna write a proposal to the RBC?"

"We'll send it from the Council of Elders to Jack, and he can put the money part together and present it."

"We don't have a Council of Elders."

"We do now," said Pearl.

My sister and I have lived apart for some years now, she in Ladyslipper House and I next door with my husband, Freddie, and our son, Skyler Vernon, whose first name was chosen by Freddie and his second by me.

Ladyslipper House is now the name of the home where Rain and I lived with Dolly and Vernon, and it has changed from how it looked when we first saw it the day we moved in. The year before Dolly died, it became a group home, owned by the Mozhay Point Band with some financial assistance and loans from several sources, including the Minogeezhik Trust, established by Mrs. Minogeezhik's late husband, Frank, and managed by Joseph Gallette, Artense's younger brother. The kitchen now opens onto an addition at the back of the house, which has almost doubled the size of the building; the dining room and front room have been converted to bedrooms and Junior's pantry bedroom to an office, and a roof now shelters the deck. The backyard ends at a new garage and storage shed, and the residents, usually six in number and always female, keep a vegetable garden at one side of the yard and a bank of flowers along the other. Spruced up by some new white siding and a picket fence but with the front door in the same shade of balsam green that Vernon painted during our last week of high school and his last week to walk on the Earth, the place looks like home. Kim Dulebohn is the supervisor of Ladyslipper House, and Rainy sleeps in the bedroom she and I used to share, which she now has to herself.

Early afternoons are quiet at Ladyslipper House. Rainy and the other girls, as she calls them, although just one is young enough to still be considered a girl outside of the group home, are taking their afternoon rests; most are sleeping, lulled by the sounds of the dishwasher in the kitchen and the cooking show that is on at low volume in the multipurpose living room that opens off the kitchen. My part-time shift, 1:00–5:00 p.m., five days a week, is under Kim's supervision, and she is the unofficial mother of the house, energetic and sharp like Dolly, and like Dolly, a smoker. I am the "mother's helper," also known as the housekeeper/nursing assistant/medical records keeper/dispenser of meds—welcome here yet still an outsider to Kim's cozy, carefully planned home and family. It's a little early at the moment for after-naptime Stretch and Smile, to which I have a standing invitation from Rainy, who is as skinny and limber as she was at sixteen and laughs every time I try to touch my toes after reaching for the stars.

Once Rain and her girlfriends wake, we will gather in the multipurpose room to stretch and smile with Kim; next on the daily schedule is the residents' work time. Rain's detail is the new pantry, built into one corner of the remodeled kitchen, which she keeps clean and neat. Today, Tuesday, is mop-and-sweep-the-floor day. She doesn't mind the work, for which she is paid with spending money, and enjoys the company of the housekeeper—me—who does the heavier cleaning and the ordering from the grocery store. Help and companionship alongside work detail is always a big deal at Ladyslipper House. A housekeeper who stretches and smiles with the "girls" on the living room floor and then dust-mops the pantry floor and reads the expiration dates on boxes and cans of food under the supervision of one of the residents is extra special. That's me: extra special.

It feels good in Rainy's and my old bedroom, where she is napping and where I walk with the Swiffer, gliding it back and forth under her bed before sitting in the little white-painted chair next to her bed.

"Rain?" I whisper. "Little sister, *ginibaa ina, nishimay?*"

What makes one child survive and one not? And at what point in the heaviness of grief did Rain stop moving forward and fall behind as I continued to run? I ask myself this, trying to imagine by pretending that I am my little, older sister who I address as *nishimay*, little sibling, as I stroke her hair, soothing her to wakefulness.

She looks like the child to whose beginnings she is returning in her dementia. This could be her second chance at childhood; not many get to do that, and I hope that the revisit will wipe out some of what surely is left in her soul from the first. Stroking her hair I think that if I absorb her traumas into myself, she will be at peace, that I must have space for them somewhere and will never be at peace myself anyway. Here is little Rainfall Dawn at four, so small that she is often mistaken for a toddler, living with Loretta and me in the apartment on First Street, both of us back with our mother—it would be forever, she promised. Rainy, thin with those birdlike bones and blackened teeth that hurt, who drops her glass bottle of Kool-Aid on the floor of the apartment because she is afraid of the man who is shouting at Loretta, and the bottle breaks on the ceramic tiles in front of the blocked-off fireplace, which distracts the man, whose fist dents the wall, cheap drywall that has divided off part of the once-large front room into a bedroom. The sound of glass shattering, the spatter of liquid and shiny slivers from the bottle up onto Rainy's shirt and diaper, her face and hands and her legs, red that is red as blood and horrifying to the little girl, who shrieks. Was that the moment, unnoticed by Loretta, who runs out the door and down the stairs to the street? And unnoticed as well by the three-year-old who was me, Azure Sky, who said to her bigger little sister, "Stand still, don't walk," and who spreads Loretta's sweatshirt over the mess and takes Rain's hand to lead her safely to the couch. The man ran out the door and down the stairs, where he and Loretta shouted at one another until someone called the police, who found Rainfall Dawn and Azure Sky sitting calmly on the couch watching *One Life to Live*.

There is a scene that plays in my head sometimes, of the day that Loretta surrendered us to the County. The social worker has taken Rainy from our mother's arms and carried her into the elevator at the County building. She pushes a button, and the elevator doors close on the last time we see Loretta; she is standing watching the doors close and doing nothing to save us and bring us back to the apartment where she had promised we would live forever. Rain squirms, turns her head, opens her mouth to speak, but then the doors have closed and she is silent.

Separated for so long after that, I only have memories of a jumbled, dull cloudiness without Rain—though as I have become older, a memory has emerged from that smoke, a dream memory about myself at five years old, and takes place in the dark middle of the night. Azure at five who has to pee and never wets the bed tiptoes on bare feet over a dusty linoleum floor to the bathroom where, when she reaches in the pitch blackness for the porcelain tank to ascertain where the bowl is, she touches skin, the knees of a man who sits on the toilet. He has been waiting for her. "Close the door, Azure," he said, "and come in."

And earlier than that: Azure at four is tall for her age, tall enough to look out the bathroom window where leaves fall from the trees to the dry grass of the backyard, where they are picked up by the wind to dry swirls that spin once, twice, then scatter under the light of a shining silver moon. The toilet tank fills, stops when the float reaches the waterline, and then she hears the heavy, dusty whisper of bare feet on the hallway. The door opens; he holds the knob to silence the sound of its closing. He is large, the bottom button of his pajama shirt is unfastened; his belly bulges from the gap and hangs over his pajama pants, his navel a flattened silver dollar lit by moonlight, which it reflects.

I try not to imagine where Rain was during that time. Once we were reunited, I pretended that we would be ourselves again, Azure Sky and Rainfall Dawn, wounded and battered but each beginning to brighten a little more every day, reflecting the other's light until we shone like the northern lights from our memory of Loretta dancing on the fire escape that night of the memory that just might be real. I made myself believe that—at Sherry's, and even at Mrs. Kukonen's, a mean and stingy placement but better than separation from Rain, and then at Dolly's and Junior's, who hoped to return us both to what we should have been, Anishinaabi-oshkinikwe, cared for and even spoiled a little.

But as Rainy sat in the beautifully curved chair in Chief Miletich's office that afternoon long ago, were his words, spoken with sympathy and kindness, the point at which she gave up? I didn't see it.

The front door bell chimes; because Kim spends early afternoons in the office on the endless paperwork and reports that are involved with running a group home, I leave my still-sleeping sister to see who is there. Looking in through the floral semifrosted window is my husband, Freddie Simon, the residents' favorite guest. Guests, no matter if they visit every day or occasionally, are always a big deal at Ladyslipper, but the girls are especially fond of Freddie because he never seems to tire of playing cards or board games. Rain has lately been asking for his help with the pantry inventory, trying to hide her ever-increasing confusion about which cans are fruit and which are vegetable, hoping that Freddie has not noticed, or at least will not call it to my attention. I see it, of course, as I have seen for months: that she cannot tell the difference between shampoo and liquid soap in the shower, between the dust mop and her memory of a fluffy, small Yorkie of the same size and shape.

My sister is failing, she lives in a group home, we do the best we can with the hand we have been dealt.

"Hello, boss; how long are you going to work today?" Freddie is proud of what we have done for Rainy, the group home next door to our own house, out of which he runs his computer consulting business. "Did you have lunch? Any of that chicken salad left?" He fixes himself a plate, conscientiously choosing cucumber slices instead of bread, on his never-ending quest to lose twenty pounds, and turns the television on the kitchen counter to a news station, with the volume just above a whisper.

In her room Rainy is curled up on her single bed, on top of the sheets and covered by Junior's green-and-black-plaid Pendleton blanket, given to her on a rainy late afternoon not long after we arrived at his and Dolly's house. That afternoon we had been sitting on the porch watching the rain and waiting for Junior to drive Dolly home from work. We had planned to go to Sammy's for a pizza and then to a football game at Denfeld but had heard on the radio that it had been canceled. When the car pulled up in front of the house, Dolly ran from it to the porch, with her jacket hood pulled over her head.

"Aren't you getting damp? Did Jennifer go potty?" she asked.

We were, and Jennifer had, with me holding the umbrella over her while she did her business, as was Jennifer's habit when it rained. "The game's canceled—can we still go to Sammy's?"

"Yes, but give me two minutes to use the biffy, and I've got to call Sis."

Junior walked to the porch slowly as was his habit in heat, sun, rain, or snow, and stood next to our lawn chairs, watching the rain with us. "Rain, your lips are blue. Are you freezing?"

"A little."

He went inside the house and came out with his camping blanket, which he kept folded in his tiny pantry/sewing room/bedroom as an extra layer for cold nights. "Here." He draped it around Rainy's shoulders.

"Migwech," said Rain, which made Junior smile.

"You can keep it," he said.

"Your good blanket? I'll keep it forever!" said Rain, which made Junior smile again.

This afternoon Junior's camping blanket, now so soft from wear and love that it has lost its woolly scratchiness, wraps from around Rain's skinny backside to a gathered wad that she holds tightly to her chest and chin. Although the blanket has been dry-cleaned many times, it still holds the scent of coffee, Jean Naté, and faint cigarette smoke from Dolly's cozy homemaking; of the baby shampoo Dolly used on her Yorkie, Jennifer; of the sand at the Curve, the beach near the bus stop along the way to Park Point, which just below its sun-dried surface smelled of the dampness of rotting wood and fish.

Up until I was fourteen and Rain fifteen, my sister, the great need of her soul rooted in the earth of our ancestors, was a flower that turned its face in the direction of where the sun, our mother, should be. Since then, however, Rain has slept with her face turned to the west, where if she is no longer alive our mother might have walked, and where perhaps in that place so far away in the next world she in turn dreams of us.

She is waking, slowly as she always does. On the wall in Rainy's bedroom is an enlarged print of a picture booth photo, a reminder of what our mother and Auntie Artense looked like at five. Since we cannot remember her face, what we have has become imprinted onto the memories that we grasp, not really caring if they are real or made up. The picture booth photo, in a birch-bark frame made by Freddie's father, is the one tangible memory we have, somewhat blurred by the enlargement process at Duluth Photo.

Rainy thinks the photo is of the two of us, Azure Sky and Rain-fall Dawn, when we were little girls.

By the summer of 2012, when Rain was thirty-nine and I thirty-seven, my little big sister had become fearful of the bath towel left mounded on the bathroom floor, of the gleaming purple grape jelly that oozed from her sandwich that I had cut diagonally, of the flocking black crows surrounding the bird feeder that Kim had hung from the eave over her bedroom window. The dust mop that had been to Rain a little Yorkie named Jennifer had become a hairy insect; behind each cupboard door in the pantry that had been Junior's bedroom lurked shadow beings who stared at Rain from between cans of beef barley soup and boxes of Cheerios with eyes the color of air. And on the early evening of the heavy rain that became the summer flood of 2012, those beings scrabbled on the roof of the white-sided house with the Tannenbaum Green front door, their curved, rain-colored claws scattering the tiniest ice balls of hail as they ran back and forth above Rain's head, their soaked tails slapping on the shingles.

Brittany, the college student who helped part-time with evening duties, called. Nadine, the overnight shift worker, had asked her to tell me that Rain had been unable to sleep and seemed unsettled and now said that she wanted to go outside. Could I come over for just a little while to talk with her and help her feel a little better?

Rain was waiting inside the front door when Brittany buzzed me in, wearing her windbreaker over her pajamas and carrying her yoga mat. "Can I bum a ride to the coffee shop?" she asked, and then, "Where's Azure?" her untied shoelaces skittering on the hallway floor as she dodged past me and out onto the porch. Outside, she ran down the sidewalk to the picket fence, where I caught up to her as she rattled the gate back and forth; it was, as it always was, locked. She pulled the hood of her windbreaker up over her head, turned, and then froze—mesmerized by the small tree at the curb, a maple recently planted by Freddie and just the size of a person covered by wet leaves reflecting in the streetlights. She knelt. "Who is it, who is it?" she asked.

I held out my hand, which she grasped, rising to her feet.

"It's so dark out here, Azh," she said.

Back at Ladyslipper House we hung our soaked jackets over the backs of two stools at the kitchen counter, and then I heated water for hot chocolate while Rainy changed into dry pajamas. We watched the Weather Channel with Nadine and Brittany, the college girl soothing Rain with chatter about her new kitten, her fondness for grilled cheese sandwiches, and the scarf she was learning to crochet, until the end of her shift at ten o'clock. Rain, calmed by the mostly one-sided conversation, or perhaps bored, blinked sleepily; Brittany, by instinct or nature, kept talking.

"It's a good night to stay inside, isn't it?" Brittany asked Rain as she put on her jacket. "I am going to really sleep tonight—I love listening to the rain on the roof, don't you?" Rain looked nervous. "Do you want my *People* magazine to look at before you go to bed? I can get it back when I see you tomorrow."

"Do you have to go?"

"I have to go check on how the little kitty is doing—I'll be back right after supper tomorrow, and we can take a look to see what the garden looks like. I bet we'll have a lot of cleaning up to do out there!"

"It's so dark outside."

"Nadine and Azure will watch me while I walk out to the car, won't you, guys?"

"We will, for sure—I always watch out for you girls," answered Nadine.

"Will you take a picture of the kitty to show me?" asked Rain.

"Sure—and when she is a little bigger, maybe she can come for a visit."

I walked with Rain to her bedroom, where in the dim light from the hallway she turned back the quilt on the wall side of the bed where she had slept since we moved into Dolly and Junior's house. "Brittany's nice, isn't she?" she asked as she slid her feet into the sheets and turned the pillow top to bottom then side to side, as was her habit. "Do you think she has a sister?"

"You will have to ask her tomorrow when she comes in to work."

"I hope she does. I hope she has a sister like you. Azh? Tell me the story about the northern lights before you go; you know, the one where the lights sang and our mother danced."

I sat in the small white glider chair next to my big little sister's bed and turned on the bedside lamp, a small pink ginger jar with a lavender shade similar to the one Dolly had bought when she fixed up Junior's bedroom for us.

"Well, it was when we lived in that apartment downtown, the one with the fireplace and the colored glass flowers across the top of the front room window . . ."

"The one with the scary bathtub down the hall and the mean lady?"

"Oh, she wasn't so mean—and remember, our mother washed us up at the kitchen sink so we didn't have to go into the bathtub, and outside the kitchen door there was a little porch."

"With stairs, remember?"

"Yes, stairs up above and below, and our mother woke us up that night and brought us out to the little porch to see the northern lights. And she wrapped us in a blanket so that we wouldn't get cold."

"And the lights were singing to us, and then she got up and danced. Remember, Azh?"

"I remember that. I do."

After Rain fell asleep I checked on the other residents with Nadine, pausing at each bedroom door where they were open just an inch or so, and looked inside at the sleeping girls. Then we walked through the house looking for any leaks from the roof or around the windows, or seepage in the basement, listening for the sump pump to hum and rattle as it worked its magic, then I left Ladyslipper for home next door. In the darkened dining room, Freddie was talking quietly over a headset to a customer, his face lit an eerie blue from the computer screen. He covered the mouthpiece and said, "Hey, babe" before turning back to his work. I stepped out of my shoes and hung my jacket by the front door, then sank into the recliner next to his work table. I stretched out my legs, resting my feet on his lap. He absently rubbed them while I listened to the rain and closed my eyes.

Drifting to the sound of rain driven by wind I saw it: Miller Creek in Lincoln Park swelling and rising, finally rushing, water seeking its own heaviness against a crack in one of the largest rocks lining the sides of the creek, its pressure building deep inside the crack where it loosened the ice that had formed there ten thousand years ago, when the water had receded and created the basin below the Skyline that is Onigamiising, Duluth, the place of the small portage.

I felt the weight and pressure in my dream, rain on rain, a torrent that overflowed the banks of Miller Creek, gushing over the outcropping of rock next to the footbridge, finding its way into the center of the largest boulder, abandoned by any living creatures of Lincoln Park since the night that Loretta disappeared. Rain filled the crack that had been expanding there for a million years or more—the boulder watching and waiting to meet me in my dream since its underwater days. Above ground the boulder had cracked and expanded over countless thaws and freezes; inside, it had become a shelter for hibernating bears in winter. The autumn that Loretta disappeared, the bears didn't return, instead traveling westward by night along the railroad tracks and across the boulder-studded Skyline Drive to the rock outcropping above the eons-old waterline.

In the recliner I turned, turned in my sleep. From a great distance I felt Freddie pat my foot, spread a fleece blanket over my shoulders and arms.

"I'm going next door to see how the sump pump is holding up," he whispered. "Our basement is dry so far." He closed the back door quietly on his way outside, his key clicking reassuringly as he turned the lock to keep us safe, me and Skyler.

Outside, the headlights of a car turning the corner onto our street sent a brightness across the front room window that caused me to open my eyes. The dark window sparkled, spattered with raindrops reflecting the moving light, and I found myself looking into Auntie Girlie's dark purple, glittering eyes. She in turn met the longing of my spirit directly. I understood the moment to be extraordinary, and not only because her gaze came from the spirit world: we Anishinaabeg ordinarily address one another in a delicately oblique fashion. So, Auntie Girlie, what do you want?

"Boozhoo, Auntie," I began wordlessly. "Aniin ezhiya-yayaan?"

"Oh, mino; ni mino ayaa. Giin dash?"

"Gaye niin, Auntie."

Auntie Girlie's spirit took a deep breath. Rain droplets, blown by the wind, danced and joined, forming larger drops that, glowing, ran down the window in rivulets.

"You have work to do, my girl. We are proud of you." Behind Girlie, the ikwewag spirits of Grandmother Maggie and Great-Grandmother Artense nodded as she spoke. "Keep it up; keep going. Know that we are with you."

As the car proceeded down the street, the reflected raindrops of Auntie Girlie's eyes vanished from my sight. Hoping another car might light the window again, I reached, reached, and brushing my hair back from my face I saw the torrent of water pouring from between the ancient cracked rocks of the bears' abandoned shelter that surrendered its secret, the body of a young woman that was then borne on the current down the creek, down, down through Lincoln Park and the underpass on Third Street, rising for a moment in back of the house on Second Street where Artense and Loretta had played as little girls the summer before they began school, then back underground, borne in the darkness to St. Louis Bay at the far western end of Duluth. She surfaced, afloat on the rapid of waters in the bay westward, westward, until she disappeared from my sight.

· · ·

I woke, slowly, to the pop and snap of popcorn in the microwave, the tearing sound of the bag being opened, the dry sound of popped corn poured into a plastic bowl. Opening my eyes I looked, as I always did, out the window that faced Ladyslipper House and saw that the desk lamp in the activity room was on, where Nadine was probably lightly napping or, perhaps, reading Brittany's *People* magazine.

"Are you awake, Mom? We made a bedtime snack; want some?" Skyler stood outlined in the kitchen doorway, holding a large plastic bowl and a bottle of apple juice; behind him, Freddie carried three Tupperware plastic bell glasses and a small stack of paper napkins. Their soft hair, cut in the neat buzz favored by both, stood up in gentle spikes on the tops of their heads, adding an inch of height to both.

"I'd love some," I said. *Gog dash gogoons, my porcupines, how I love you,* I thought.

LINDA LEGARDE GROVER is a professor of American Indian studies at the University of Minnesota Duluth and a member of the Bois Forte Band of Ojibwe. Her short fiction collection *The Dance Boots* received the Flannery O'Connor Award for Short Fiction and the Janet Heidinger Kafka Prize; her collection of poetry, *The Sky Watched: Poems of Ojibwe Lives*, was given the Red Mountain Press Editor's Award and the Northeastern Minnesota Book Award for Poetry; and her novel *The Road Back to Sweetgrass* (Minnesota, 2014) won the Wordcraft Circle of Native Writers and Storytellers Fiction Award. Her book *Onigamiising: Seasons of an Ojibwe Year* (Minnesota, 2017) received a Minnesota Book Award and the Northeastern Minnesota Book Award for Memoir/Creative Nonfiction.